Aspirin & Elephants

A Romantic Comedy in Two Acts

by Jerry Mayer

A SAMUEL FRENCH ACTING EDITION

SAMUEL FRENCH

FOUNDED 1830

New York Hollywood London Toronto

SAMUELFRENCH.COM

ISBN   978-0-573-69354-0   Printed in U.S.A.   **#3587**

TO DEAR AND BUDDY

IMPORTANT BILLING AND CREDIT
REQUIREMENTS

Aspirin & Elephants was originally presented at Santa Monica Playhouse (Chris DeCarlo and Evelyn Rudie, Artistic Directors). in Santa Monica, Ca, produced by Emily Bettman Mayer and Santa Monica Playhouse, on July 14th, 1989. It was directed by Chris DeCarlo; the set design was by Scott Heineman; the lighting and sound was by Evelyn Rudie; wardrobe by Kay Borgsmuller and the production stage manager was George Vennes. The cast, in order of appearance, was as follows:

HONEY (RUTH FRANK). ....Priscilla Morrill
JUNIOR (STEVEN FRANK) ....William Schallert
STEPHANIE GALE .... Sandra Kerns
SCOTT GALE.....................................Vince McKewin
ARNIE NATHAN ....Todd Susman
LIZ NATHAN ....Susan Cash
VOICE OF CAPTAIN NORDENKJELL.....Robert Easton
VOICE of RUSSIAN TOUR GUIDE.......... Bella Susman

Aspirin & Elephants subsequently opened at The American Stage Company in January 1992. It was directed by Jim Dale; the scenic design was by Scott Heineman and Gordon Danielli; the lighting design by Ted Mather; the sound design by Bruce Ellman; the costume design by Barbara A. Bell and the production stage manager was Mary Ellen Allison. The cast, in order of appearance, was as follows:

HONEY (RUTH FRANK) ....Natalie Ross
JUNIOR (STEVEN FRANK) ....Sam Coppola
STEPHANIE GALE ....Laura Sametz
SCOTT GALE...Mark Nassar
ARNIE NATHAN ....Ted Neustadt
LIZ NATHAN ....Eliza Ventura

CHARACTERS

These are upper middle-class Midwesterners. They're neither ethnic, nor WASPish, they're somewhere in the middle, St. Louis. These are real identifiable people and they are at their funniest and most moving, when they are played for reality.

HONEY FRANK: Late fifties. She's attractive, warm, elegant and very much in love with Steven Frank Jr., her husband of forty years. She runs her household and charity projects like a "Press Secretary," smoothly and capably. Honey is "Hepburn" to Junior's "Tracy" and a close friend to her two daughters.

STEVEN FRANK JR. ("JUNIOR"): Early sixties. Junior is appealing and masculine, a guy everyone likes. He owns a men's clothing manufacturing firm and because of his rough charm he's equally at ease with loading dock foreman and department store head.
Note: JUNIOR. had a heart attack three months ago. It's important that he never appears whiny or self pitying. Rather, he's a lion with a thorn in his paw.

LIZ NATHAN: Mid thirties, Liz is the capable, no nonsense daughter, who is attractive but not as stunning as her sister Stephanie. She's intelligent, bluntly honest and confident that she can get any job done. Despite all this, she's appealing and fun.

ARNIE NATHAN: Late thirties, a diamond in the rough. Arnie's a struggling comedy writer fighting for self-esteem as a writer and as a son-in-law. He has obviously "married up," but not because he's a social climber, he's just crazy about Liz. We are continually aware of Arnie's appetites, both sexual and gastronomical.

STEPHANIE GALE: Mid thirties, a knockout. She's a "Princess" but not an airhead. Stephanie has lots of undiscovered potential which she discovers during the course of the play. There's substance to Stephanie, even though at first she seems materialistic and narcissistic, because she's trying too hard to win her husband's love.

SCOTT GALE: Scott, forty, is Ivy League handsome, successful and, above all, competitive. He makes a contest out of everything from drinking, to running his lingerie firm more profitably than his father did, to making Stephanie constantly come to him for affection. It's important not to play Scott too contemptibly. Remember, he thinks he's funny, likable and above all, a winner.

TIME

The present, during the summer.

PLACE

The luxury cruise ship "Royal Norway," on a cruise from Copenhagen to St. Petersburg and back again.

(Scenes flow continuously without stopping)

ACT I

(LIGHTS COME UP on the luxury liner sitting room of Honey and Junior's suite. The decor is Scandinavian, Nordic art and oak. The bedroom is through a door, Stage Right. The fourth wall faces the room's veranda and the sea. Liz's room and Stephanie's room will be created with the use of lighting, in the sitting room, at center stage. HONEY FRANK, pretty, well dressed, sixty, enters. SHE takes six brown pill bottles from her purse and puts them on the bar.)

CAPTAIN'S VOICE. *(SPEAKER. A slight Norwegian accent.)* This is your Captain, Haak [Hock.] Nordenkjell, welcoming all passengers aboard the Royal Norway. Soon, we will be leaving Copenhagen to begin our exciting Scandinavia/Russia Cruise. So we kindly request all visitors to now depart the ship. Thank you, or as we say in Norwegian, "Tak." We will be under way in twenty minutes.

HONEY. *(Shocked at the announcement.)* What!? Over my dead body! *(SHE dials the phone, talks.)* Reception? This is Mrs. Stephen Frank Jr. in Cabin 112, Atlantic Deck. Have Mr. and Mrs. Arnold Nathan checked in yet? He's my son-in-law. —I know I have a son-in-law already on board, Mr. Gale. Mr. Nathan is my *other* son-in-law. He and my daughter are flying in from Los Angeles to join the cruise. The ship won't leave exactly on time?—In

9

exactly nineteen minutes.—Couldn't you at least take your time pulling up the anchor?

JUNIOR. (*O.S.*) Honey, where the hell are you?

HONEY. (*Into the phone.*) Even five minutes would help. (*Calling toward the door.*) I'm in here, Stateroom One twelve. Just stay out in the passageway with the bags, dear. (*Into the phone.*) Sir, it's very important that my husband avoid stress. I alerted your ship's doctor of his recent heart attack. If my daughter and son-in-law miss the boat it might just ...

(*HONEY, her back to the door, doesn't see JUNIOR FRANK enter and overhear her.*)

JUNIOR. Kill the old geezer

HONEY. (*Shocked.*) *Oh*, you *shit*! (*Into the phone, quickly.*) I *beg* your pardon. You've been very helpful. Goodbye. (*To Junior.*) Don't get upset, they'll make it.

(*JUNIOR FRANK, 60, is attractive, athletic, well dressed, "a man's man," with a dry sense of humor. His hand unconsciously in his shirt, is subtle evidence of his heart attack, three months ago.*)

JUNIOR. Who's upset, if they miss the boat I'll save a small fortune.

HONEY. I told Liz to be here an hour early. Here's your pillow. (*SHE hands him a tubular neck pillow.*) I'm sure Arnie's making them both late. He can be so inconsiderate.

JUNIOR. Honey, I'm not gonna spend this whole trip waiting around for the little bastard. And he's gonna learn that quick. Because you're going to tell him.

HONEY. Right, that's my department. By the way, what's *your* department?

JUNIOR. Being lovable and trying not to fart at the Captain's table. (*Noticing the row of brown bottles.*) You sure you brought the thousands of pills it takes to keep me alive?

HONEY. (*Patiently, touching the bottles.*) Right here, and it's only hundreds.

JUNIOR. (*HE picks up bottles, checks labels.*) Beta blockers, Digitalis, Valium, Aspirin, Dalmane, Cardizime and Egg Foo Yung with lobster sauce.

HONEY. (*SHE laughs.*) Isn't this a wonderful suite? Nice big bedroom in there and we have our own veranda.

JUNIOR. (*HE walks up the steps.*) What the hell's this, an obstacle course?

HONEY.Two little steps. Rubin said exercise is good for you.

JUNIOR. Try to convince my ticker of that. (*HE feels his heart.*)The unreliable little son-of-a-bitch.

HONEY. Your heart is not unreliable.

JUNIOR. (*HE lights a cigarette, his back to her.*) Right, it's a real workhorse. That's why I had a major coronary from tearing open a pack of tomato seeds. Next time, one good sneeze and goodbye.

HONEY. There isn't going to be a next time. (*SHE sees him smoking.*) Junior, don't make me hurt you!

JUNIOR. One puff and I only exhaled. The kids are late, I'm very upset. (*HE puts the cigarette out.*)

HONEY. You fraud. Be right back. (*SHE exits.*)

JUNIOR. You wouldn't take away my last remaining pleasure.

(HONEY enters carrying two bags.)

JUNIOR. Honey, what are you doing? Let one of those *Olafs* do that.

HONEY. It's only our carry-on things. I've got to do something with my hands, since my son-in-law's *neck* isn't here.

JUNIOR. You're forcing me to help you. You realize that the wife carrying the bags can be a very castrating experience? *(HE grabs an O.S. bag, pulls it in.)*

HONEY. Not if you treat it maturely.

JUNIOR. I mean for *you*. And you *know* I like my women ballsy.

HONEY. Good, then I'll order you around a little. Here, it's your aspirin day. *(SHE hands him water and aspirin.)*

JUNIOR. Are you sure they have a doctor on this bucket?

HONEY. I told you, there's an excellent ship's doctor.

JUNIOR. What does a Norwegian doctor know about a St. Louis heart attack? And how the hell am I gonna complain? The only Norwegian words I know are herring and Sonja Henie.

HONEY. Just complain in English, like you always do to me. Dr. Sardenfjord will understand you.

JUNIOR. Dr. *What*?

HONEY. Sardenfjord.

JUNIOR. Great, while I'm trying to pronounce his name, I'll *croak*. This is a big ship. What if Dr. Sardinehead can't find me?

HONEY. I'll paint arrows from his cabin to yours. You *could* move in with him?

JUNIOR. He might demand sexual favors. At least *you* know better. (*HE exits to bedroom.*)

HONEY. (*SHE picks up phone, dials.*) I'm calling Stephanie and tell her to stand out by the gangplank and watch for Liz.

(*As HONEY dials her phone, A SPOT comes up on Stephanie's cabin.*

HONEY. *Dammit*, busy.

(*HONEY exits to bedroom. LIGHTS CROSSFADE to Stephanie's room. The PHONE is ringing. STEPHANIE, pretty, well-dressed, 35, enters and picks up the phone.*)

STEPHANIE. Hello. Yes, Scott Gale of Slumbertown Sleepwear is here. Who's calling? —*Oh*? One minute please. (*Calling O.S., with an attitude.*) Scott, Bloomingdale's Lingerie Department, calling, from New York.

(*SCOTT, 40, an attractive yuppie business type, enters carrying a drink.*)

SCOTT. Really?

STEPHANIE. Don't act surprised. How could you have her call you here?

SCOTT. (*HE holds hand out impatiently.*) Stephanie, the *phone*. That's Bloomingdale's! If you lose that call!

(SHE hands him the phone. As HE talks, SHE places things from her shopping bag in drawers under the beds, listening.)

SCOTT. Hello?—Marci. Hi, how did you track me down in Copenhagen?—Well, it's sweet of you to wish me bon "voyahge," but you know what I really want to hear. Did you like my new baby dolls and teddies?—Fabulous.— Of course I'll embroider "Bloomies" on your teddies. Any old place you like. (*HE bursts out laughing.*) That's a very good place.—*Sure* I can deliver right away. I brought my portable FAX with me. FAX me your order and I'll FAX it right back. Marci, really, you've *made* my trip. Thanks, Babe. Bye bye. (*HE hangs up triumphantly.*) I got Bloomingdale's, the Big B, and I did it all on my own. The best Dad ever got was Gimbels. The buyer loves my line.

STEPHANIE. And you seem to love the buyer's line. You FAX *Marci*, Marci FAX *you.*

SCOTT. Stephie, Stephie, how many times are we going to go through this? Would you feel better if women were barred from business schools?

STEPHANIE. No, I'd feel better if Marci hadn't answered the phone in your hotel room on your last trip to New York.

SCOTT. I am insulted. If you'd just once, try to understand my business. Lingerie buyers *always* come up to the manufacturer's hotel room to look at samples.

STEPHANIE. At eight in the morning?

SCOTT. (*Innocently.*) When necessary. You've got to get up early to make a buck. You'd know that if you ever worked for a living.

STEPHANIE. I *do* work for a living. At something even more important than baby dolls and teddies. Raising our two sons.

SCOTT. Please don't cry. You know your face puffs up like a blowfish.

STEPHANIE. I am not crying.

SCOTT. Stephi, knowing my boys are at home with a terrific mom like you totally frees me mentally. You're like part of my sales team.

STEPHANIE. Yeah, I give great peace of mind.

SCOTT. And don't worry about Marci, she's fat and unattractive. You know I insist on beauty. That's why I married you.

STEPHANIE. You're just saying that to make me feel better.

SCOTT. Of course, but it's true.

STEPHANIE. You know how much I'd like to believe you. Scott, I want this cruise to be really wonderful for us, and healing.

SCOTT. It'll be one big band-aid.

STEPHANIE. And as a favor to me, could you hold down your drinking a little?

SCOTT. Sure. (*HE smiles, lowers his glass.*) How's this?

STEPHANIE. Perfect. Moonlight on the ocean is just what we need. (*SHE kisses him.*) It's time to get back to the thing that made us fall in love in the first place. (*SCOTT's back is to the audience. SHE squeezes a cheek of his ass.*)

SCOTT. (*Dryly.*) My wallet's in the other pocket.

STEPHANIE. You louse!

(SHE exits, HE'S right behind her.)

SCOTT. I was *kidding.*

(LIGHTS CROSSFADE to Honey's room as HONEY, then JUNIOR enter from bedroom.)

HONEY. I don't believe this, the ship leaves in eight minutes and they're not here. It's typical of Arnie, but not Liz.

(The PHONE rings, SHE grabs it.)

HONEY. Stephanie, are you aware that your sister still isn't … —*Arnie!* Where on earth are you, dear? (*Listens, then for Junior's benefit.*) In the reception area! Thank God!—Well I wasn't really worried that you'd miss the boat, but you did call it close this time. Did Liz make it too? Good, let me talk to her. (*A beat, till Liz gets on.*) Liz, sweetheart, we weren't sure you were joining us.—I see. (*To Junior covering the phone.*) Arnie *had* to stop for Danish pancakes with lingonberries on the way from the airport. (*Into the phone.*) Yes, Daddy's right here, he's fine, he's *dying* to see you.

JUNIOR. Nice choice of words.

HONEY. Just dump your stuff and come up to the Atlantic deck, Room 112.—I can't wait either. Bye. (*SHE hangs up the phone.*) Well, they made it.

JUNIOR. (*HE sits, SHE joins him.*) Of course they made it. The little bastard's not gonna pass up thirteen free days of sun, sea and "All you can eat."

HONEY. Junior, I really think it's a bad habit, calling our sons-in-law "The Little Bastards."

JUNIOR. I never called them that to their face. Actually, I like the little bastards. Of course I'm not wild about the way Arnie hugs me all the time. Since they moved to Hollywood, he thinks he's Zorba the Greek.

HONEY. (*Hugging him with warmth, enthusiasm.*) It must be hell to be so huggable. Isn't this a great way to celebrate our anniversary? Don't you feel better, just being on this wonderful ship, with the whole family, going to St. Petersburg?

JUNIOR. (*A quick kiss on her lips, then:*) Nope. Should I lie or tell you the truth?

HONEY. You couldn't lie if you tried.

JUNIOR. I'm feeling kind of shaky. I don't tell you every time I get one of these little flip-flops in here. (*HE puts his hand inside his shirt.*) Or a twinge in my left arm.

HONEY. Rubin said just take a nitroglycerin. He recommended this cruise. There are other heart patients on it.

JUNIOR. Yeah, "The Ship of Wimps." And you read about that helicopter crashing?

HONEY. That was a news helicopter. Medical helicopters don't take any chances. Anyway, we're not going to need one.

JUNIOR. What if something happens when we're a hundred miles out to sea in one of those fjucking fjords? (*JUNIOR exits into the bedroom.*)

HONEY. Those ... fjords aren't as wide as the Mississippi. Just try to relax. (*SHE exits to the bedroom.*)

(LIGHTS CROSSFADE to Liz's cabin. LIZ NATHAN, organized, attractive, mid-thirties, followed by ARNIE NATHAN, a comedy presence, late thirties, enter. THEY are dressed in sweatsuits, carrying luggage. HE has a portable typewriter.)

ARNIE. I do *not* make you late for everything.

LIZ. Really? What about almost missing our flight at L-A-X? Running like demented people from the cab to the plane, with you knocking that poor old woman down?

ARNIE. I did not knock her down. I spun her around a few times.

LIZ. We should've left home earlier.

ARNIE. How could we, with Dad on long distance screaming his final job offer at me?

LIZ. Are you telling me he won't wait for your answer till we get back from our trip?

ARNIE. That's what I'm telling you. Unless I misinterpreted the expression, "Shit or get off the pot!" *(Looking disdainfully around the cabin.)* God, this cabin is *tiny.* Weren't there any larger rooms?

LIZ. Yes, deluxe doubles, for twelve hundred dollars more. Daddy wanted to splurge and pay extra, but I wouldn't hear of it.

ARNIE. *I'd* hear of it! Liz, aren't you kept busy enough, just being cheap for yourself? How are the two of us gonna fit on that bed? Two *Ethiopians* couldn't fit on that bed.

LIZ. Arnie, starvation jokes are not funny!

ARNIE. That wasn't a "starvation joke." That was a "thin joke." Okay, borderline taste, I admit it. Impending sexual frustration does that to me.

LIZ. There won't be any frustration.

ARNIE. Are you crazy! We're sleeping apart. Our erogenous zones are gonna be at right angles to each other! (*HE demonstrates, with his hands.*) How are we gonna, where the hell will we...?

LIZ. Screw?

ARNIE. Funny. Go ahead, talk dirty. That's the only thing you *can* do dirty in these beds. Unless you're the Flying Walendas.

LIZ. We'll be just fine. Come here. We've had some very sexy evenings in single beds, remember? (*SHE draws him down onto the bed.*)

ARNIE. Yeah, but we were single at the time, *anything* was sexy.

LIZ. Arnie, you know it has the opposite effect on me, when you get psychotic about sex.

ARNIE. I'm not psychotic, I'm *practical*. It's not that romantic at home these days, with Jimmy walking in on us in the middle of things.

LIZ. I know, it's awful. We'll try locking our bedroom again. Maybe he's over his bad dreams.

ARNIE. Or at least let me sprinkle some carpet tacks in the hall, to give us an early warning system.

LIZ. (*Amused.*) You will not. By the way, our room's next to Stephie and Scott's. Isn't that neat?

ARNIE. Fabulous. He just better not start with his "How's it going out in Hollywood *guy*?" Which means, "How much did you make last year *guy*?" *Don't* tell him it was fourteen thousand.

LIZ. Of course not. It's none of his business. And it was twelve-two after they deducted health plan and retirement.

ARNIE. Thanks for being so exact. Don't tell Scott I write "Mugsy Magruder" either.

LIZ. Will you stop feeling ashamed of Mugsy? Just consider it a building block to the better things you're going to do. (*SHE snaps his photo with a small camera that she uses often, like an offensive weapon, on everyone.*)

ARNIE. I left St. Louis talking about all the great movies I was gonna write, and I end up writing Saturday morning kiddie poo, for peanuts. If it weren't for your bookkeeping job, we'd be starving.

LIZ. Well we're not starving. And good things are gonna happen. (*SHE sprays her mouth, then his with Binaca.*)

ARNIE. I'll tell you what's gonna happen. I'm gonna cable Dad and tell him I'm ready to come back to St. Louis.

LIZ. *Arnie,* we're not making that decision yet!

ARNIE. Why not? There's a lot worse ways to earn a living than ... (*His face reflects his attitude.*) the pest control business. Dad promised I won't have to deal with rats.

LIZ. Why don't we discuss this later? They're expecting us upstairs. Can we go?

ARNIE. With pleasure. Suddenly I'm claustrophobic.

LIZ. (*A gentle hint.*) I *know* the feeling.

ARNIE. How am I gonna write a script in this crypt? (*Looking around.*) Y'know, they say you're born with prenatal womb memory. They're right. This is the place. (*To the room.*) See ya later, Mom.

(THEY exit, LIGHTS CROSSFADE to Honey's cabin. We hear KNOCKING on the door.)

STEPHANIE *(O.S. Excited.)* Honey, it's Stephanie. Quick, let me in.

(HONEY enters from the bedroom, crossing to the door. JUNIOR follows.)

HONEY. Is something wrong?

(HONEY opens the door and STEPHANIE enters with a shopping bag marked "COPENHAGEN." SCOTT follows, with a half-finished drink and a small lingerie box.)

STEPHANIE. Of course not. I organized our shopping and got it all done in an hour. Found a fabulous store, "Scandia Arts." I bought fanny packs for us girls. *(SHE pulls out fanny packs.)* I bargained them to their knees, Daddy. Only three bucks each.
JUNIOR. Jesus, I pay that just for zippers. I'm gonna hire you as a buyer.

(STEPHANIE hands HONEY a fanny pack.)

HONEY. Thank you Stephie, it's stunning.
SCOTT. And I brought you a little gift from our New York showroom. *(HE opens the box.)* Our biggest selling nightshirt. 100% cotton, "Spring Rose Pattern."
HONEY. Oh, I love it. Thank you, Scott. *(SHE kisses him.)*

SCOTT. My pleasure. See, it comes with a little pocket.

JUNIOR. Handy, she can keep her birth control pills in there.

(LIZ enters, followed by ARNIE.)

LIZ. Hi! Got room for another daughter?

(EVERYONE ad libs squeals, hugs and warm greetings. Dialogue overlaps. This is a family that enjoys kidding each other.)

LIZ. Sorry we were late.

HONEY. *(Lightly.)* Oh, it doesn't matter.

JUNIOR. *(HE reacts to her hypocrisy.)* It doesn't matter? She was chug-a-lugging my heart medicine.

ARNIE. Junior, how are you? *(HE gives Junior a big hug.)*

JUNIOR. Fine, Arnie. You've gotten stronger.

SCOTT. Arnie, how you doing, guy? *(HE offers his hand in an affected "Ivy League" manner, palm down.)*

ARNIE. Just great, guy. *(ARNIE shakes Scott's hand and drifts off to the bedroom.)*

LIZ. Daddy, I've missed you so much. How are you feeling?

JUNIOR. Not bad, daughter. Nothing a burial at sea wouldn't fix.

LIZ. Stop that. I smell cigarette smoke on you!

JUNIOR. One puff.

STEPHANIE. His so-called doctor, Rubin Fry, allows him to smoke.

JUNIOR. Only when my daughters make me nervous.
(*HE shakes his hand nervously.*)

LIZ. Daddy, can't you be serious for a moment?

JUNIOR. Nope. That's your mother's department.

ARNIE. (*Enters from the bedroom.*) Nice bedroom. Is
that bed queen size?

HONEY. King.

ARNIE. (*For Liz's benefit.*) King? King size.

JUNIOR. Honey, where the hell's my medicine? And
make sure it's that Russian vodka, Archeecharnya.

HONEY. You mean Stolichnaya?

JUNIOR. I hate a smartass bartender.

HONEY. I'm pouring Archeecharnya for everybody.

SCOTT. Make mine a double.

STEPHANIE. Liz, you're positively skinny.

LIZ. Thanks, I lost three pounds. (*Kiddingly.*) And you
haven't *gained* that much.

STEPHANIE. (*Acting insulted.*) That's a nice thing to
say after I bought a fanny pack for your skinny ass.

JUNIOR. (*To Honey.*) I am shocked at their language.
You allow that kind of shit?

HONEY. I gave up years ago.

STEPHANIE. Daddy, we know you wanted sons.
That's why we force ourselves to talk dirty.

JUNIOR. Sure I wanted sons, so they could support me
in my old age, which is *now*.

SCOTT. Nice sweatsuit, Arnie.

ARNIE. Thanks.

SCOTT. What is that, 65% polyester? Next time try
100% cotton. Much classier.

ARNIE. Nah, I hear 100% cotton shrinks your shvanzheimer. (*HE strides in "well hung" pride.*) Not that that worries *me*.

JUNIOR. Honey, do I have my blasting caps?

HONEY. In your shirt pocket. (*Slightly concerned.*) You don't *need* one?

JUNIOR. (*Checking a pill box in his shirt pocket.*) No, just keeping my nurse sharp.

ARNIE. Blasting caps?

HONEY. Nitroglycerin tablets, in case Junior has some mild discomfort.

JUNIOR. Oh yeah, mild discomfort, like elephants tap dancing on my chest.

HONEY. Elephants are not allowed on this ship. Here's your drink. (*SHE hands JUNIOR a drink.*)

LIZ. (*Re Junior's drink.*) Mother, isn't that awfully strong for Daddy?

HONEY. It's mostly tonic.

JUNIOR. (*Raising his glass.*) A little toast here. First, glad to have you aboard. Thanks for joining us.

(The KIDS chuckle, ad lib "Glad to be here." "Anytime." "Here here.")

JUNIOR. There are just two rules I'd like to see observed. One, your money's no good here. All the food's free and I want you to sign for drinks.

(LIZ snaps his photo. HE poses patiently.)

JUNIOR. Two, I don't want to be hearing "Thank you Mother and Daddy" all through the trip. So get down on your knees now and get it out of your systems.

(THEY laugh.)

ARNIE. *(Toasting.)* Here's to rich fathers-in-law. Don't leave home without one.

JUNIOR. *(Toasting back.)* Here's to your Shvanzheimer.

(THEY drink, STEPHANIE sees Scott's glass.)

SCOTT. Steph, why don't you tell everyone our news about Bloomingdale's? You're part of my sales team. *(To everyone.)* Don't worry, she didn't buy anything, I sold something.

STEPHANIE. *(Proudly.)* He sure did. His whole winter line. They just called from New York to tell him.

JUNIOR. *(Mock concern.)* Not collect? *(Then smiling, shakes Scott's hand.)* Just kidding. Congratulations and collect your money fast. The bigger they are, the longer they take to pay.

(HONEY and LIZ ad lib congratulations.)

ARNIE. *(Toasting Scott.)* Nice going.

SCOTT. Thanks, guy. Yeah, it's a big deal. Kind of like if you wrote "The Godfather One, Two and Three." Know what I mean?

(HE drinks, ARNIE nods sickly.)

ARNIE. Yeah, guy.

STEPHANIE. Scott, is that straight vodka?

SCOTT. I haven't checked its sexual preference. What are you, the vodka sheriff?

HONEY. Junior, would you be a darling and go to reception desk and get all the passports?

JUNIOR. Yes, Captain Bligh. Next she'll have me swabbing the decks.

ARNIE. I'll tag along. Don't we go right by that Viking Smorgasbord?

SCOTT. (*To Stephanie.*) And the bar?

(The GUYS exit.)

LIZ. (*Calling O.S.*) Arnie, remember your family's fat genes.

HONEY. Now let's catch up.

LIZ. Daddy looks awful!

STEPHANIE. He does not.

LIZ. I mean he's handsome, he's Daddy. But he shuffles along like an old man. And he orders you around like you're his nurse.

HONEY. He's a little frightened. Who wouldn't be? I still check to see if he's breathing at least fifty times a night. Last week I was checking him and he opened his eyes and said, "*Boo!*" (*SHE smiles shakes her head.*) He'll be fine.

LIZ. *If* we can get him to change doctors. That idiot Rubin Fry. How can you let Daddy stay with a cardiologist who has emphysema and still smokes?

HONEY. Rubin is an old friend. You know how Daddy is about loyalty.

LIZ. But he shouldn't be allowed one puff. And I'll bet Rubin doesn't make him exercise.

HONEY. Try to make Stephan Frank Jr. do anything.

LIZ. Well he's at least got to follow some rules on food. He loves potato chips and they're like murder weapons.

HONEY. I haven't pointed a potato chip at him in a long time.

LIZ. Here, I brought him an article from *American Health.* (*SHE hands Honey the article.*)

HONEY. Fat clogged arteries in *color.* He'll treasure this. Girls, I need your help. I'm trying to get Daddy back to work, for his own good. He's not a man who can retire at sixty-two.

STEPHANIE. Mother's right, whenever I come by, he's always in front of the TV.

LIZ. Have you tried threatening him with brussels sprouts? That always got *us* out of the house.

HONEY. Of *course,* why didn't I think of that?

LIZ. Listen, while we're alone, I've got a big news flash for you. I'm *not* pregnant.

STEPHANIE. Well what?

LIZ. I've been offered a job in Production Estimating at Walt Disney Studios.

STEPHANIE. Oh my God!

HONEY. Liz, that's marvelous. (*HONEY hugs Liz.*)

LIZ. I was dying to tell you. I start next month at lots more money than I'm making now and my opportunities are wide open.

HONEY. I am so proud of you.

LIZ. But it's between us. You can't tell Daddy or Scott. Because Arnie doesn't know yet.

STEPHANIE. Why not?

LIZ. Well, uh, I'm going to surprise him ... when the timing's right. Which it isn't right now.

STEPHANIE. Lizzy how important is it, keeping your little Disney secret?

LIZ. Stephanie, don't mess around.

STEPHANIE. I won't say a thing, *if* I can send my little monsters out to L.A. to stay with you next summer.

LIZ. That's *blackmail*, twerp, you wouldn't *dare*.

STEPHANIE. Wouldn't I?

HONEY. *Children.*

LIZ. You rat, I'll *kill* you, if you even *hint*!

(THE GUYS enter, ARNIE nibbling appetizers.)

JUNIOR. We ran into the purser, they don't give the passports back till tomorrow morning.

HONEY. That's right, I forgot. Sorry, my love.

JUNIOR. No problem. I like that we're both going senile together.

STEPHANIE. *(Mischievously, to Arnie.)* Arnie, we have to talk.

HONEY. *(To stop Stephanie.) Stephanie!* Guess what, I brought along my books on The Hermitage Museum, from my art appreciation class.

STEPHANIE. Nice. *(To Arnie, who's showing interest.)* Arn, I have *so* much to tell you.

ARNIE. Yeah?

HONEY. (*Grabs Stephanie ushers her out.*) Come on, why wait till we get to St. Petersburg. I'll show them to you now.

LIZ. (*To Stephanie, making a fist.*) Yeah, I'll show you a few things too.

STEPHANIE. We'll talk later Arnie. (*Singing.*) HI HO, HI HO, IT'S OFF TO WORK WE GO.

(And the WOMEN are gone.)

JUNIOR. (*HE sits down wearily.*) Well, that was my exercise for the day.

SCOTT. Y'know, you're really looking good, Junior. How you feeling?

JUNIOR. Fair to shitty.

SCOTT. Well at least you're still functioning.

JUNIOR. Yeah, I'm putting one foot in front of the other. And if that ever changes, I'll still have things under control.

SCOTT. What do you mean?

JUNIOR. (*Conspiratorial.*) This is just between us, okay?

(The GUYS ad lib agreement, as HE pulls out a pink capsule.)

JUNIOR. I got this from my friend Rubin Fry. One of those pills they give spies before they go behind enemy lines. When life stops being fun you just bite. He calls it "The Terminator."

ARNIE. (*HE looks at the pill.*) Jesus Christ, I thought it was a "Good and Plenty!"

SCOTT. Don't even joke about doing something like that. Your insurance won't be worth a dime.

(JUNIOR reacts.)

ARNIE. Junior, suicide is not a smart idea. I don't see you often enough as it *is.* (*HE chuckles at his joke.*) Seriously, we'd miss you a lot. (*ARNIE gives him a heartfelt hug.*)

JUNIOR. Thanks, Arnie. So Scott, how's your winter line doing?

(JUNIOR breaks the hug. As HE turns ARNIE pats him on the behind.)

SCOTT. *Very* strong Junior. Bloomingdale's is practically turning their lingerie department over to me.

JUNIOR. That's not hard to take. Arnie, how's your writing going?

ARNIE. Just great, Junior. I've got a bunch of new ideas and I ...

SCOTT. (*Rolling on, to Junior.*) I created this new label, "Miss Princeton, traditional sleepwear." It appeals to a much more upwardly mobile woman than our Slumbertown label.

JUNIOR. Sounds good. A new design?

SCOTT. New for us. What I did was, I borrowed Ralph Lauren's traditional look, and a touch of Calvin Klein's love-child look, but at a *price.* And I had the whole line designed roomier, so women will feel good about themselves. A gal who's a "medium" will fit into our "small." A "large" will fit into our "medium." And a *tank* will fit into our "large."

JUNIOR. Clever.

SCOTT. Yeah. I make a lot of money off women. It's nice that I can help their self-esteem.

ARNIE. Sounds like your dad's giving you a lot to do.

SCOTT. (*Insulted and proud.*) Dad doesn't give me things to do. *I'm* president of Slumbertown.

ARNIE. (*HE laughs.*) I'm sorry, but you sounded like a Munchkin. (*A gruff Munchkinlike voice.*) *I'm* president of Slumbertown.

JUNIOR. Scott, I envy your dad. He's lucky to have a son working alongside him.

SCOTT. Yeah, except these days he's playing more golf than working. Just as well. Lingerie is a young man's business now. (*To Arnie.*) So, how's it going out in Hollywood, guy?

ARNIE. Just great, guy. I'm working on a script right now, they're gonna grab outta my hands and shoot as soon as I get back.

JUNIOR. For which show? I watch a lot of TV these days.

SCOTT. Probably that "Mugsy Magruder," right?

ARNIE. (*HE reacts.*) Yeah, how'd you know that?

SCOTT. Donny was watching TV one Saturday morning, and all of a sudden he yells, "Look, Uncle Arnie wrote this!" So we watched it. Cute, you've really got the lingo down. "Holy Mackinoly, Fluffo." (*Smiling, to Junior.*) Fluffo's her little dog. We got a goddam Hollywood writer in the family. I'll bet you make a mint out there, writing that stuff.

ARNIE. Yeah, Liz tells me I'm going through the roof.

SCOTT. And I hear she's doing well, too. Nothing wrong with a little combined income, huh guy?

JUNIOR. Yeah, Honey has yet to bring in her first dime.

SCOTT. Arn, how about a few games of shuffleboard later?

ARNIE. I've never played shuffleboard.

SCOTT. Who has? We'll learn together. Buck a point.

ARNIE. You got it

(THE WOMEN enter in conversation.)

LIZ. *(Gives Junior a box.)* This is for you, Daddy.

JUNIOR. Oh yeah? What is it?

HONEY *(SHE knows what's in it.)* You'll find out if you open it.

JUNIOR. *(HE opens the box finds a Captains cap.)* Hey, great. From the gang at the office. *(HE puts the hat on, HE allows LIZ to snap a photo, then reads a note.)* "O Captain, our Captain, Here's wishing you and your family a wonderful cruise. And then please hurry back to us. We *need* you. Love, your loyal crew." That's nice.

STEPHANIE. I'll bet they miss you plenty.

ARNIE. Hell yes.

LIZ. You'd better get back to work, so you can pay for this trip.

ARNIE. Hell yes.

JUNIOR. I'm not going back. I'm selling the company.

HONEY. *Sweetheart?*

JUNIOR. I was going to talk to you about it.

HONEY. I would hope so.

JUNIOR. You know United Textiles has been after me to sell. And I've been thinking, what am I holding on for? It's not like I have a son in the business.

HONEY. All right sell if you want to. But you told me United wants you to stay on as president.

JUNIOR. Honey, I'm not interested in being president of anything but my tomato garden.

(We hear the BELL TONE.)

CAPTAIN'S VOICE. *(SPEAKER.)* This is Captain Nordenjkell speaking. Ladies and gentlemen, for your safety, we will now have our instructive lifeboat drill. If you would kindly return to your cabins and put on your life jackets, then proceed in five minutes to your designated lifeboat station on the Promenade Deck. Tak.

(The dialogue below starts midway through the MESSAGE.)

LIZ. How do we know which is our lifeboat?

HONEY. There's a sign on your wall. Junior, I'll get our jackets. *(HONEY exits to the bedroom.)*

(ARNIE and LIZ exit.).

STEPHANIE. *(To Scott after the Captain's announcement.)* Why don't we leave our drinks here? We're coming right back.

SCOTT. I'll just hang on to mine.

STEPHANIE. *Scott!*

SCOTT. *(Smiling.)* Yes my little "stress factory?"

STEPHANIE. Can't you go without a drink for five minutes?!

SCOTT. Of course. Be right with you. (*SCOTT puts his drink down.*) Junior, I brought my portable FAX with me, in case I have to piss out some fires back at my office. Feel free to use it.

JUNIOR. Thanks Scott, but my long distance pissing days are over.

SCOTT. By the way, I got together with your fabric people in New York. Thanks for arranging it.

JUNIOR. Glad to help.

(HONEY enters, hands Junior a life jacket, then exits to get her own.)

SCOTT. You could do me another huge favor. I've got to meet with those pricks at the union when I get back. Could you give me a few pointers later?

JUNIOR. Sure Scott, any time.

(HE has trouble getting his life jacket on. SCOTT helps him.)

SCOTT. They seem to love you. This'll be my first labor contract and I don't want to go in there acting like a putz.

JUNIOR. Don't worry, you won't be acting. (*Quickly, off Scott's reaction.*) I'm *kidding*. Never give me an opening like that.

SCOTT. Good, we'll talk later. Thanks. (*HE picks up his drink and exits.*)

HONEY. Junior, I'd like to discuss this big decision you've made?

JUNIOR. (*Trying to fasten his life vest.*) I can't. I'm busy saving my life here.

HONEY. You know Rubin wants you to return to work. He says you're almost back to full strength.

JUNIOR. (*No longer joking.*) *Bullshit.* Pardon my French. I'm getting bushed just dealing with this thing. I can see myself trying to run an all-day sales meeting, popping pills, laying down every few minutes.

HONEY. Well then don't start with a full schedule. They need you down there. And you know you love to inspire people.

JUNIOR. Unfortunately I'm out of the inspiration business. Can we drop the subject for now? (*HE takes a nitro.*)

HONEY. You have pain?

JUNIOR. No, but tightness. And I'm winded.

HONEY. (*Helping him with his vest.*) Let me help you with that.

JUNIOR. Thanks, I appreciate it. (*HE kisses her on the cheek.*) Y'know, Stephanie and Scott sure seem to be getting on each other's nerves.

HONEY. I know. And he's always so charming to us. Why can't he save a little of that for her?

JUNIOR. For one thing, he isn't sleeping with us.

HONEY. He isn't sleeping with *her* either, at least not often enough, according to what Stephanie tells Liz and Liz tells me.

(*SHE starts to exit, HE follows.*)

JUNIOR. Why that little bastard! See how easy it rolls off the tongue? Jesus, things change. Who ever thought I'd be furious at a guy because he *wasn't* screwing my daughter?

(LIGHTS CROSSFADE to Stephanie's room. SCOTT enters, removing his life jacket. STEPHANIE follows. SCOTT is sullen.)

STEPHANIE. I was not trying to make you look bad in front of Honey and Daddy. But do you have any idea how many drinks you've had today?

SCOTT. I don't need a scorekeeper, I need a wife. Do I slur my words? Do I knock things over?

STEPHANIE. No. But we haven't seen each other in almost two weeks. And I'm feeling very romantic. And you're not the most attentive lover when you're smashed.

SCOTT. The girls I fantasize about when I make love to you, think I'm great.

STEPHANIE. Fantasies are a lot less demanding than real life. They don't require a sustained erection.

SCOTT. When did I *ever* fail to sustain?

STEPHANIE. When*ever* you fall asleep on me.

SCOTT Keeping me up is your job.

STEPHANIE. *(SHE picks up the bottle of vodka.)* Well *this* doesn't make my job any easier. *(SHE exits to a closet.)*

SCOTT. I just went through a really tough market week. I think I've earned the right to have a couple of drinks.

STEPHANIE. *(O.S. Sincerely.)* Scott, I know market week isn't easy.

SCOTT. It took every trick in the book to outdo those Jap firms. I showed 'em where they can shove their fucking robots. And while I was at it, I broke last year's sales record. (*SHE enters holding an evening dress.*)

STEPHANIE. Really? Well that's terrific, Scott.

SCOTT. But am I the conquering hero? *No,* I'm a *drunk.*

STEPHANIE. I didn't call you a drunk. Let's not start again. (*SHE holds up the dress.*) Do you like this?

SCOTT. You think it's easy earning the money it takes to put you in dresses like that? And to buy you your Mercedes?

STEPHANIE. I know you work hard.

SCOTT. And to pay for the new house and the club and the kids' private school and your maids?

STEPHANIE. You've made your point, Scott.

SCOTT. It costs a lot of money to spoil you. For every dollar you spend, I've got to earn twice that much.

STEPHANIE. You only tell me that ten times a day!

SCOTT. Because *you* keep *forgetting* it! (*HE exits.*)

STEPHANIE. (*SHE grabs a Vodka bottle, follows him.*) For God's sake. *Here* have a drink.

(*LIGHTS UP on Liz's cabin. LIZ, with tiny plastic bride and groom, and ARNIE, brushing his teeth, enter.*
NOTE: *The kids' cabins are on opposite sides of the stage, but during the following short scenes, feel free to intermingle the characters because they're not aware of each other.*)

LIZ. The pastry chef was so cooperative. He's baking a cute little wedding cake out of oat bran. We'll put the original Honey and Daddy on top. Have you written the song yet?

ARNIE. No. I've been trying to think of a Mugsy idea. Anyway, "Humoresque" is impossible to write funny to.

LIZ. No it isn't. Write it, please. It'll put me in a *very* warm mood. You know what I'm saying?

ARNIE. Yes, I know what you're saying. You're saying you'll do it for a song. Why don't you and Stephanie write it?

LIZ. No *Arnie,* we're not clever, we're *cute.* And you've always been so good at writing adorable anniversary songs.

ARNIE. I *hate* writing adorable anniversary songs. It makes me feel like a talented amateur. Then I have to watch Scott smirk and ask me when I'm moving back to St. Louis.

LIZ. Don't listen to him. Believe me, Scott admires you plenty for doing exactly what you want to do with your life.

(SCOTT and STEPHANIE enter their area.)

SCOTT. Arnie really looked pathetic in that outfit, didn't he? "The Prince of Polyester."

STEPHANIE. I thought he looked nice.

LIZ. What did you think of Stephanie's new hair?

ARNIE. Interesting. How does she do that, with a dustbuster?

SCOTT. It's obvious Arnie's not making it on the coast. He's not even writing prime time.

STEPHANIE. Liz says he's doing fine. *(STEPHANIE exits.)*

SCOTT. What else is she gonna say? Look at the facts. He's been out there almost three years and they still live in an apartment in the *Valley*. Everyone with an ounce of brains and a nickel in his pocket bought a house in Beverly Hills. We need ice. (*SCOTT exits with the ice bucket.*)

ARNIE. What am I doing here? Our baby sitter makes more money than I do and I'm cruising the North Sea.

LIZ. The *Baltic*. And for God's sake, enjoy it.

ARNIE. How? Every time your parents look at me I feel like a freeloader. It's common knowledge they didn't want you to marry me.

LIZ. It's not common knowledge. Only *we* and *they* know it. And that was sixteen years ago. They're crazy about you now.

ARNIE. That's a laugh. I move their daughter two thousand miles away so I can start a new career, now *you're* supporting *me*.

LIZ. Not true. We're working side-by-side and I love it.

ARNIE. And Scott's knocking 'em dead. He's president of "Slumbertown," he's earning a fortune, and he's making his dad look like a senile putz. That's every goal he ever set. By the way, I need some money.

LIZ. What happened to that thirty dollars I gave you before?

ARNIE. Shuffleboard with Scott happened!

LIZ. Oh, Arnie.

ARNIE. (*A rueful request.*) Please give me money!

(*LIZ exits, ARNIE follows. STEPHANIE, in low-cut dress, and SCOTT enter.*)

STEPHANIE. You think this dress shows too much Stephanie?

SCOTT. No, it's good. Let 'em drool.—I've been thinking about you and Liz. You are so lucky.

STEPHANIE. I know, she got math skills, I got cleavage.

SCOTT. You know what I mean. She has to work because Arnie's not cutting it.

STEPHANIE. Liz is having a ball, working. And Arnie's making progress. Writing's a tough field, just like yours.

SCOTT. Shit, how can you compare Arnie's situation to mine? I'm taking off like a rocket and he's in the denial period of his failure.

STEPHANIE. Scott, isn't it enough that you succeed? Does everyone else have to fail? Why must you be so damn competitive?

SCOTT. You mean, why must I be a *winner*?

STEPHANIE. There are things more important than winning. Like having compassion and being a good person. (*STEPHANIE exits.*)

SCOTT. (*Dismayed.*) Oh my God, is that what you're teaching our boys? (*SCOTT exits.*)

LIZ. (*Enters, talking O.S.*) Arnie, there's something I want to talk to you about.

ARNIE. (*Enters, shaving with a cordless razor.*) Y'know, the only smart decision I've made lately is buying this cordless razor. So I don't have to look in the mirror when I shave. I bought our stocks too high, I sold our house in St. Louis too low. Then I buy you a Tojo, the only Japanese car that ever went bankrupt.

LIZ. (*SHE takes his razor, shuts it off.*) It's pronounced "To-Jee-O" and I'm going to run you down with it if you don't stop this self-flagellation routine.

ARNIE. Okay, I'll take a break. What did you want to tell me?

LIZ. Nothing, it's not important.

ARNIE. No, you've been acting like something's on your mind. Go ahead, I can take any news, except that you're having an affair with Woody Allen.

LIZ. I just wanted to tell you ... to loosen up, relax.

ARNIE. Relax? How? I've gotta come up with a Mugsy Magruder script and I can't even think of a story for the little bitch. *Wait* a minute. "Little bitch?" What if Mugsy's dog Fluffo falls in love with a little bitch and runs away from home. Hold it, Fluffo's a female dog too. I wonder, is Saturday morning ready for a story about gay dogs? I think so.

LIZ. You'll think of a story. Come here, I'll inspire you. (*SHE'S on a bed, motions him over.*)

ARNIE. Is there room? (*HE gets on top, kisses her.*) Not bad, if you like "Love, Quasimodo style." Which I *do.* How much time before dinner?

LIZ. Not enough. (*SHE rises, exits to the closet.*)

ARNIE. Don't you want to unblock me? Quasimodo, fast little fella.

LIZ. (*O.S.*) Sorry Quas, later. Get dressed.

ARNIE. It'll be your fault if I get a hump on my *front* too.

LIZ. (*SHE enters, hands him a sportcoat, exits.*) We'll deal with that. Here, wear your seersucker tonight. You look very handsome in it.

ARNIE. (*HE checks the inside label.*) *Shit.* Fifty-five percent polyester. If Scott tries to read my label, I'm gonna grab his solid gold Mark Cross pen and take his temperature with it.

(ARNIE exits. SCOTT enters, STEPHANIE hanging on his back.)

SCOTT. Will you get off my back?

STEPHANIE. Not until you mellow out. You're a wonderful businessman, a fabulous tennis player and a terrific skier. And I won't mention your drinking again, okay?

SCOTT. Okay.

STEPHANIE. I've layed out a marvelous evening for us.

SCOTT. Good, keep us organized. Otherwise we might relax.

STEPHANIE. You'll love this. After a light dinner, an hour's gambling in the casino, followed by a ten minute stroll around the deck. And then back here, for Courvoissier, caviar and *us*.

SCOTT. Terrific. What time am I scheduled for a sustained erection?

(THE LIGHTS CROSSFADE to Honey's room. We hear BELL TONES.)

CAPTAIN'S VOICE. (*SPEAKER.*) This is Captain Nordenkjell at the end of a very pleasant first day on our Scandinavia/Russia cruise. I do hope you all enjoyed the "Dance with your Captain Party" in the Midnight Sun

Lounge. It was my pleasure to meet and dance with so many of you, particularly the ladies. (*HE chuckles.*) May I wish you all a goodnight. Tak.

(HONEY and JUNIOR enter.)

HONEY. Wasn't that fun?

JUNIOR. Sure, for *you.* You were dancing and flirting with Dr. Sardinehead all night.

HONEY. I meant it was fun having the kids with us. And I wasn't flirting with Sardinehead. We had one dance.

JUNIOR. Hey kid, I've got radar, the hairs on the back of my neck.

HONEY. He simply wanted to introduce himself and tell us that he'd received your medical records from St. Louis.

JUNIOR. Oh, that's why he kept referring to you as "The Widow Frank." (*As HE exits to the bedroom.*) Classy, they turned down the bed.

HONEY. Guess what I brought along?

(HONEY turns on a small tape recorder.
We hear "their song." [Any romantic "standard" we'll all
know and love.] JUNIOR enters with two small green-
wrapped mints.)

JUNIOR. Our song. Aren't you the sneaky one? Mints on our pillows. Probably only an extra hundred bucks.

HONEY. You wouldn't dance in the Viking Lounge. How about here?

JUNIOR. You're determined to give me a treadmill test. Okay a little dancing, very little.

(THEY dance. HONEY enjoys it dreamily.)

HONEY. I just want to be in the arms of the handsomest man on the Royal Norway.

JUNIOR. Sorry kid, you're stuck with *me.*

(THEY shuffle around. HONEY spins, holding the outstretched arm of an almost unmoving JUNIOR. SHE bends backwards.)

HONEY. Dip me?

JUNIOR. Not unless I send out for help.

HONEY. *(Snuggling up.)* Remember that Bachelor's Ball you took me to, and that drive home in your father's Packard? And those creaky stairs leading up to my bedroom?

JUNIOR. Oh my God, you're getting horny.

HONEY. No, I'm just reminiscing.

JUNIOR. Then I'm getting horny. One of us is definitely getting horny.

HONEY. You want to do something about it?

JUNIOR. Yeah, let's eat our mints.

HONEY. You realize of course that chocolate is supposed to be an aphrodisiac.

JUNIOR. Just eat the green part. Listen, I think it's only fair to tell you, I found the book.

HONEY. What book?

JUNIOR. You know what book. *(HE produces a book from a drawer.)* "X Rate Your Heart Attack. Performance anxiety, libido failure."

HONEY. Oh, that book? Stephanie gave me that.

JUNIOR. You've been discussing our problem with the girls?

HONEY. Of course not. And we don't have a problem. The book was an unsolicited gift, like Liz's "Oat Bran Cook Book." The girls just want to be helpful.

JUNIOR. (*HE opens the book.*) Here's a helpful chapter, "Humping keeps Your Heart Pumping." (*HE flips the pages.*) And this one, "Comfortable positions for 're-entry.'" At first I thought it was a guidebook for astronauts.

HONEY. We don't need any guide books. You're the only guide I've ever needed. And the best. Of course I have no basis for comparison. But that's what you've always told me.

JUNIOR. And you've always bought it.

HONEY. I'm still buying it. (*SHE kisses him tenderly.*)

JUNIOR. Maybe we *are* ready for the chocolate part.

(*THEY exit to the O.S. bedroom. As THEY leave, JUNIOR tosses the book into the waste basket. A few notes of "their song" swell up as LIGHTS CROSSFADE to Liz's cabin. LIZ enters, followed by ARNIE, eating from a plate of pastries.*)

LIZ. How can you say that Daddy wasn't depressed? (*SHE starts undressing.*)

ARNIE. You're making such a big deal out of the fact that he didn't feel like dancing. (*HE offers her a pastry.*) Butterdeig? That's pastry in Norwegian.

LIZ. (*SHE shakes her head.*) It's not just that. His whole attitude is so negative.

ARNIE. He was just a little quiet that's all. (*Offering her a chocolate.*) Sjokolade? Chocolate's one of those words that's the same in every language, like toilet.

LIZ. How can you eat, we just had dinner?

ARNIE. I'm an oral person.

LIZ. He's so listless and withdrawn.

ARNIE. You don't just bounce back overnight from a heart attack.

LIZ. Now he doesn't even want to go back to work. And he's so helpless and self pitying. And Honey's completely permissive. She's got to lay down some rules. He's becoming a textbook cardiac cripple. (*SHE'S now in her bra and slip.*)

ARNIE. Sweetheart, relax. Junior's gonna be fine. Which bed do you like best?

LIZ. I don't care. I can sleep on either one.

ARNIE. Who's talking about sleeping?

(*HE kisses her. SHE's impatient.*)

LIZ. I'm sorry, I just can't concentrate right now.

ARNIE. (*HE munches on her neck.*) That's all right, I'll concentrate, you let your mind wander.

LIZ. Arnie, *really,* I have never felt quite so out of the mood. I'm dead tired and I'm worried about Daddy. You can understand that. (*LIZ exits carrying her clothes.*)

ARNIE. Hey, he invited us here to have a good time. You don't want him to waste his money? (*HE pulls his necktie straight off. It's the clip-on variety.*)

LIZ. Arnie, I just don't feel like it. Can't you bear with me on this? (*LIZ enters ready for bed.*)

ARNIE. Of course I'll bear with you. Who *else* am I going to bear with? It's not that crucial that *I* may be under some stress too, from a slight career crisis, that is tightening like a noose around my scrotal area. Sure, no problem, I'll bear with you.

LIZ. All right, if it's *really* that important. (*After a beat, long sufferingly.*) I'll take care of *you.*

ARNIE. You'll take care of *me*? What *is* this, "Tuneup Masters?" In other words, you'll give me a hand?

LIZ. You don't have to be gross.

ARNIE. I'm sorry, but the only thing I find worse than no sex, is mechanical sex. But thanks anyway for offering to "take care of me," Mrs. Goodwrench.

LIZ. I am not Mrs. Goodwrench. I love making love with you. But not when you're treating sex like it's a miracle drug. Every time you have a disappointment, you get passionate and come looking for me.

ARNIE. And you're beginning to hide.

LIZ. I'm right here. But if you want me to be more excited, you've got to stop feeling sorry for yourself. Self pity is not the sexiest trait a man can have.

ARNIE. (*HE reacts.*) Can't argue with you there. That explains why I don't excite you.

LIZ. Arnie, you *do* excite me. That isn't what I ...

ARNIE. Or maybe it's your career. That might be where all your excitement's going lately. You know what I mean?

LIZ. Arnie, nothing's more exciting to me than you. I'm sorry I said that stuff. But I'm so tired.

ARNIE. Sure, you go to bed. I'll go get my *Newsweek* back from Scott and see whose career is more pathetic, mine or Donald Trump's.

(ARNIE exits. LIGHTS CROSSFADE to Stephanie's cabin and LIZ exits.
STEPHANIE is on the phone.)

STEPHANIE. *(Into the phone.)* Room Service? This is Mrs. Scott Gale in 108, Mediterranean Deck. I ordered the caviar.—No, that's why I called. I don't want you to bring it. I've changed my mind. Just cancel it, okay? Thank you.

ARNIE *(O.S.)* Scott, it's Arnie.

STEPHANIE. The door's open.

ARNIE. *(Enters.)* Hi, I saw the light under your door. I've got nothing to read. Is Scott finished with my *Newsweek*?

STEPHANIE. Scott's not here. He's still up in the casino. I saw the magazine somewhere. Come on in. *(SHE looks for the magazine.)*

ARNIE. You couldn't talk him into leaving the blackjack table? I left before you were finished arguing.

STEPHANIE. He said he's staying till he gets even. He *loves* getting even. *(SHE finds the Newsweek and Vogue.)* Here. And Liz wanted to read this *Vogue*.

ARNIE. Thanks.

STEPHANIE. I guess *I* just wasn't enough of an inducement to lure him down here. Even with Courvoissier Why don't you drink his, before I do. *(SHE gives ARNIE a glass of brandy.)*

ARNIE. Sure. Steph, are you okay?

STEPHANIE. *(SHE cries, throwing her arms around him.)* Oh, Arnie! Yes, goddamit, I'm just fine. I'm not going to cry anymore over that son-of-a-bitch! *(SHE touches her face.)* Is my face puffy?

ARNIE. Nah, it makes you look like you have high cheek bones.

STEPHANIE. Why have I always fallen in love with assholes? And then, after I'm in love with one, why does it take me so long to admit that he's an asshole? And then, why do I keep forgiving him for being an asshole?

ARNIE. Those are tough questions.

STEPHANIE. You were at our wedding, wasn't it wonderful?

ARNIE. Terrific. Those tenderloin filets were like butter.

STEPHANIE. Scott was such a handsome bridegroom. Those green eyes against his tan. He must've used a whole tube of bronzer. I was so in love. All I wanted to do in Acapulco was drink banana margaritas and screw.

ARNIE. You sound like good company to me.

STEPHANIE. Not to Scott. That's when he started to beat me.

ARNIE. What?!

STEPHANIE. At water skiing and SCUBA diving and spear fishing and anything else he could look better than me at. It wasn't a honeymoon, it was the Pan Am Games.

ARNIE. What an idiot.

STEPHANIE. Thanks, you always say the right thing. I ought to keep you around. Why wasn't I smart enough to pick a husband like you?

ARNIE. You were young and confused.

STEPHANIE. I'll bet Liz is wondering what happened to you?

ARNIE. She's sound asleep.

STEPHANIE. Good, I feel like talking. You want to hear a secret? No, I'm getting drunk, I don't know what I'm saying.

ARNIE. Oh what the hell? What's your secret?

STEPHANIE. I used to have a crush on you.

ARNIE. Really? How recently?

STEPHANIE. (*Emphatically.*) A long time ago.

ARNIE. Listen, if we're telling secrets ... I used to think ... (*HE chuckles.*) I might've married the wrong sister.

STEPHANIE. (*Sternly.*) *Arnie!* (*Then.*) How recently?

ARNIE. What time is it? God you smell good.

STEPHANIE. That's not me, It's the *Vogue*. It's full of perfume ads.

ARNIE. I'll bet you smell nice too. (*HE leans forward and sniffs.*) Yeah.

(*Suddenly SHE kisses him.*)

STEPHANIE. What am I doing? Am I crazy?

ARNIE. I try not to analyze these things.

SCOTT. (*Enters.*) Hi.

ARNIE. (*Jumps up, turns his face away slightly and shakes Scott's hand.*) Hi, Scott. I hope you don't mind me taking my *Newsweek* back. I had absolutely nothing to read.

SCOTT. Take it. I'm sure Steph has better things planned for me.

STEPHANIE. Actually, I'd given up on you. Arnie and I were just about to hop into the sack.

(*ARNIE laughs nervously.*)

SCOTT. Good, then you've got her all warmed up for me.

STEPHANIE. (*An edge of petulance.*) You must've gotten even. Why else would you have quit?

SCOTT. As a matter of fact, you're wrong. I *didn't* get even. I got *ahead.* Twelve hundred bucks. (*HE holds up a wad of bills.*)

STEPHANIE. You're kidding me! (*SHE looks at the money.*) Oh my God! You're not kidding!

ARNIE. Terrific. This is your drink, Scott. (*ARNIE hands SCOTT the brandy.*)

SCOTT. Thanks, Arn. You warmed *this* up for me too.

STEPHANIE. (*Hugging him gleefully.*) I love you! How did you get the nerve to bet that much?

SCOTT. You're born with it. Like I told you, Arnie, staying power. Told you not to pull out after you lost forty bucks.

ARNIE. Gotta remember that. Don't pull out too soon. Goodnight. (*ARNIE exits.*)

STEPHANIE. Goodnight Arnie. (*SHE sees SCOTT unbuttoning his shirt.*) Here, let me help you with that.

(*The LIGHTS CROSSFADE to Honey's cabin.*
JUNIOR enters from the bed area looking distressed,
breathing into an oxygen inhaler attached to a small
tank.)

HONEY. (*O.S.*) Junior, will you please lie down?

JUNIOR. (*HE lowers the oxygen bottle.*) Lying down is what started this problem. I'll be okay.

(HONEY enters.)

JUNIOR. I guess your kisses still take my breath away.

HONEY. I've got your pills. Do you have pain?

JUNIOR. Not yet. But it's ticking fast with some of those flip-flops. You'd better time me.

(SHE times his pulse with her watch.)

JUNIOR. *Elephant,* stay the fuck away from me. This is just great. Goddam invalid. This whole trip idea was nuts.

HONEY. No it wasn't. Rubin told you not to get overly concerned about something like this.

JUNIOR. Screw Rubin. He isn't floating around thousands of miles from a hospital. What happens if "Dumbo" decides to land on my chest?

HONEY. I'll tear his ears off. Now relax and be quiet for a minute.

(LIGHTS dim slightly and our attention shifts to Stephanie's room, too dark to really see anything.)

STEPHANIE. Darling, you want to move your arm, so there'll be a little more room? Sweetheart, your arm? Scott?!

SCOTT. Huh? What?

STEPHANIE. You son-of-a-bitch, you were *asleep!*

(SHE exits. HE follows.)

SCOTT. Maybe you're oversexed Stephanie, d'ya ever think about that?

(Honey's room. LIGHTS come up again. SHE times JUNIOR's pulse.)

HONEY. It's much slower now. Normal, really.

JUNIOR. You mean normal for a parakeet. Y'know, you really made a lousy deal, getting me.

HONEY. Best deal of my life.

JUNIOR. After three months, I'm still scared of my shadow, in *and* out of bed.

HONEY. You'd have to be crazy not to be scared. You've had a heart attack. But remember, you survived it.

JUNIOR. I don't call this surviving.

HONEY. Junior, I just know it would help for you to talk to someone.

JUNIOR. Please don't start with the shrinks again. They aren't going to convince me that this is any way to live, surrounded by medicine bottles and oxygen tanks. I ought to just stop taking the aspirin and the nitro and let nature do its housekeeping.

HONEY. You know I'm not going to let that happen.

JUNIOR. The best anniversary present I could give you, is just to walk out that door and not come back.

HONEY. Oh, Darling.—Where are you going?

JUNIOR. I'm going to put on my jacket. One of the few things I can still do by myself.

HONEY. Do you want something? I'll get it for you.

JUNIOR. I'm taking a walk, which I believe I can handle, if I don't have to climb more than two steps.

HONEY. All right where should we walk?

JUNIOR. You aren't going. I want to think things over, alone.

HONEY. I'm not letting you go out there without me!

JUNIOR. Don't make me hurt you! That's a laugh. We both know you could take me. (*HE starts to exit.*)

HONEY. (*SHE moves toward him.*) Will you please stop this!

JUNIOR. (*Firm and insistent.*) I am taking this walk alone. If you follow me, I'm going over the rail. I wasn't a bad hurdler, remember?

HONEY. (*Almost tearful.*) You've always been a wonderful hurdler. Please come right back.

JUNIOR. Sure.

(*HE kisses his fingers, waves, then exits. HONEY picks up the phone, dials.*)

HONEY. (*Into the phone.*) Amie, hi, it's Honey. Could you and Scott come up to our room? No emergency, Junior's okay. (*SHE dials another number.*) Dr. Sardenfjord? This is Mrs. Frank. Mr. Frank has experienced some palpitations. No pain, just a quickened heart beat with what he calls flip-flops.—Well ... frankly we were starting to get intimate. Just barely starting.—Yes, I timed him and he's almost back to normal. But he's depressed about it and insisted on taking a walk around the deck, by himself. I just wanted to be sure you were available, if I need you.

(*THE KIDS enter.*)

HONEY. Thank you doctor. You're very comforting. Goodnight. (*HONEY hangs up.*)

LIZ. Mother what's wrong?

HONEY. Nothing. Girls, you didn't have to come.

STEPHANIE. Where's Daddy?

HONEY. He's fine. He was feeling independent and wanted to walk around the deck. But I'd be more comfortable if the boys found him and walked along with him, that's all.

ARNIE. Sure. Where is he?

HONEY. Why don't you try the Promenade Deck first? And please call me right away when you find him.

SCOTT. Right. Let's go Arnie.

(ARNIE and SCOTT exit.)

LIZ. Honey, why didn't you go after Daddy yourself?

HONEY. I told you, he's feeling very independent. (*SHE smiles bravely.*) Now everything is fine. I don't want this to spoil the fun of the cruise.

STEPHANIE. What happened? Did you and Daddy have a fight?

HONEY. Be serious. Please girls, everything's under control. Liz, you're looking tired. (*SHE busies herself.*)

LIZ. Why don't we stay with you until Daddy gets back?

HONEY. I'd rather you both go to bed. It's very late.

(The GIRLS exchange glances.)

STEPHANIE. We'd rather keep you company.

HONEY. Girls, I'm going to insist. I'd prefer to be alone right now, really.

STEPHANIE. You're sure?

HONEY. Positive. Now give me a kiss.

LIZ. Well, okay then.

STEPHANIE. Goodnight, Honey.

(The GIRLS kiss Honey, ad lib goodnights and start to exit.)

LIZ. You will call us if you...? *(Resolutely, SHE stops.) No.* We're not leaving.

STEPHANIE. *(Thankful that Liz spoke up.) Good,* Liz.

LIZ. Mother, it won't work anymore. We're not twelve. We don't want to be protected from everything.

HONEY. I'm not protecting you.

STEPHANIE. You do it automatically. Whenever there's a problem, you become reassuring and cheerful, like a press secretary.

HONEY. Sometimes, it's a matter of privacy. Everything in my life is not open to inspection, even to my daughters.

LIZ. What kind of relationship do we have if you won't share the bad things as well as the good? We want to help.

HONEY. Well you're not helping. All you're doing is upsetting me.

STEPHANIE. Maybe we *could* help, if you'd be truthful with us, instead of giving us that brave smile we always get.

HONEY. Don't *worry*, you're not going to get a smile! Have I ever lied to either of you!

STEPHANIE. Of course not. But you're not completely honest, either. Whenever I do something you don't approve of, instead of telling me how you really feel, you say, "Do whatever you think is right, dear."

HONEY. You want me to tell you every time I feel your decisions are immature and overemotional? That will keep me very busy!

STEPHANIE. (*Taken aback.*) *Oh.*

HONEY. It's your turn Liz. When have I lied to *you*?

LIZ. It's not exactly lying, it's diplomacy. When Arnie and I got married, you never would come out and admit how you really felt about him.

HONEY. It's true, I didn't think Arnie was good enough for you. And I'm glad I didn't tell you that. Because, as it's turned out, Arnie is *plenty* good enough for you!

LIZ. Thanks.

HONEY. Is there anything *else* you want to know the truth about?

LIZ AND STEPHANIE. (*Almost together.*) Yes.

LIZ. What happened with Daddy?

HONEY. *All right,* if you won't leave me alone. Daddy and I tried to make love tonight for the first time since his heart attack. But he started getting frightened because his heart was racing. He's terrified. I am too. And he's ashamed of himself because he doesn't feel like a man anymore. (*Frustrated and undone.*) Now what the hell good did it do for me to tell you that?!

STEPHANIE. A lot of good. At least now we know the pain and frustration you're going through.

HONEY. I can handle the pain and frustration. What I can't handle is *this.*

LIZ. Mother, have you ever considered the possibility that we might actually be helpful? I've read five heart attack books since last April, and there are some basic rules they all agree on.

HONEY. *Liz*, you know what you can do with your damn rules! It's obvious you think I'm doing a lousy job of taking care of Daddy.

LIZ. I never said that.

HONEY. You didn't have to. I saw the look on your face tonight when I let Daddy order a hamburger.

LIZ. What look?

HONEY. (*Pointing at Liz's face.*) *That* look! Don't you think I know about cholesterol charts? I've memorized the damn things. But dealing with Daddy is like walking a tightrope. If he can't have a hamburger once in a while, he offers you his arm and says, "Just feed me intravenously." Then he goes off and smokes. You know Liz, you can be very patronizing and judgmental.

LIZ. Well if you don't want me to be *truthful.*

HONEY. I *don't.* And Stephanie, you're full of good advice too, which you always give me on the run, between a tennis game and a clearance sale.

STEPHANIE. That's unfair, Mother. You know I'm always there for you.

HONEY. (*Controlled frustration.*) I *know* you are Stephanie, be somewhere *else* for awhile, okay? (*"The General," totally in charge.*) *Now,* if you both want to *really* help, go out on that deck and help those little bastards find your father!

(HONEY points to the door. The GIRLS exit obediently. LIZ has another thought and comes back in. HONEY points, commanding thunderously.)

HONEY. *Go!*

(LIZ exits quickly and we FADE TO BLACK.)

CURTAIN

ACT II

LIGHTS COME UP to reveal Honey's room. JUNIOR lays on the couch, awake. We hear the three BELL TONES.

CAPTAIN'S VOICE. (*SPEAKER*.) This is Captain Nordenkjell. I'm sure you all enjoyed your nice sunny day in Oslo, "City of the Vikings." Tonight, we will sail through the Gulf of Finland to the highlight of our cruise, St. Petersburg, the "Versailles by the Sea." Tak.

(During the above, JUNIOR hears something and pretends he's asleep. HONEY then enters carrying a book and crosses to JUNIOR, leaning over him to check his breathing. JUNIOR brings one hand up and firmly grabs her behind.)

HONEY. (*Shocked, jumping back.*) Ahh!! You idiot! I'm going to stop checking you.

JUNIOR. I thought you'd be pleased to feel signs of life. Where've you been? Having a matinee with Dr. Sardinehead?

HONEY. I had a matinee with my book and a deck chair.

JUNIOR. (*HE checks his watch.*) Six fifteen, how come you're not fixing me my Archeecharnya?

HONEY. (*SHE starts making drinks.*) Coming right up.

61

(There's a KNOCK at the door.)

HONEY. It's open, come in.
LIZ. *(O.S.)* Fine, don't write the damn song.

(LIZ and ARNIE enter.)

LIZ. *(Bright and cheerful.)* Hi. Daddy, did you have fun in Oslo?
JUNIOR. I'm whipped, daughter. Your mother dragged me to some huge sculpture garden. If I never see another bronze pecker, it'll be soon enough.

(SCOTT enters with a folded tee shirt.)

LIZ. Hi, Scott. Where's Stephie?
SCOTT. She'll be right here. *(Mischievously, to Arnie.)* Hey, guy, I bought you a little gift today. *(HE tosses the tee shirt to Arnie.)*
ARNIE. Really? I didn't know you cared. *(HE displays the tee shirt.)* The University of Oslo?
SCOTT. *(Chuckling.)* Yeah, I thought you could wear that to the ship's masquerade party tomorrow night, and go as someone with an education.
ARNIE. Thanks, I'll try to remember to talk good.
STEPHANIE. *(O.S.)* Okay, Scott. I'm ready for my entrance.

SCOTT. Right. (*Announcing.*) And now, brought to you at great expense, *mine* ... "The Queen of Instant Gratification" ... Stephanie Gale.

(STEPHANIE enters, modeling her mink jacket as SCOTT sings, to "A PRETTY GIRL IS LIKE A MELODY.")

SCOTT. (*Singing.*) A PRETTY GIRL, CAN LEAD TO BANKRUPTCY.

STEPHANIE. Isn't it fabulous? Real "Norwegian Mink." The ship's store is having a sale. Do you believe only eight hundred dollars? The styling's dated, but at that price I can do some redesigning and have it altered. Liz, don't you just love it?

LIZ. (*Flatly.*) No, Stephanie, I *hate* it.

(EVERYONE reacts.)

LIZ. That shouldn't be a surprise. You know I'm president of the Valley chapter of "No Fur! No Sir!"

STEPHANIE. Oh, that? Well you're talking about *wild* animals. These are domesticated minks, raised on their own little ranch.

LIZ. You think these domesticated minks on their own little ranch enjoy having their skins ripped off and their bodies ground up into cat food?

JUNIOR. (*Repulsed.*) *Jesus*! I'm planning to have a rare hamburger tonight.

HONEY. Can we change the subject?

STEPHANIE. God, Elizabeth, you don't have to make me feel like a murderer.

LIZ. I'm being honest. To me, that isn't a jacket, it's twenty mink carcasses.

SCOTT. (*Dryly.*) *And* twenty well-fed cats.

JUNIOR. Maybe I'll try cornflakes tonight. (*HE starts to exit.*)

HONEY. Girls, you're upsetting your father.

JUNIOR. Who's upset? I'm taking a leak. (*HE exits.*)

STEPHANIE. (*To Liz, very emotional.*) You know style is important to me. I didn't hurt any animals. They were already dead.

LIZ. Stephanie, you know better than that. Be honest with yourself. Your whole life has turned into an empty, narcissistic shopping spree.

HONEY. Can we talk about something pleasant, like St. Petersburg and The Hermitage?

SCOTT. I vote for that. This is just more of Liz and Arnie's sour grapes anyway.

ARNIE. What's that supposed to mean?

SCOTT. It means, if you can't *afford* something, make the people who *can*, feel guilty, so *they* won't enjoy it either.

ARNIE. Who says we can't afford a lousy thousand bucks?

SCOTT. You either can't afford it, or somebody's too cheap to.

ARNIE. Are you calling my wife cheap!?

SCOTT. The two of you have always been critical of anything we buy that's out of your price range.

STEPHANIE. Scott, don't.

ARNIE. You don't know what our price range is. And I don't give a shit about how you waste your money. Like on your five thousand dollar Bang and Olufsen music wall.

SCOTT. Oh for Christ sake! That's *Bahng* not *Bang*.

ARNIE. How about *Bung*?!

LIZ. Please, Arnie. I'm sorry, Honey.

SCOTT. See, you're trying to make me feel guilty again. Well forget it. I believe that achievers should be rewarded. In this case, with perfect sound.

HONEY. Boys, here are your drinks. (*Firmly as SHE hands them drinks.*) *Drink*!

ARNIE. And exactly what *are* your big life achievements, guy? Other than getting your dad to make you president of his company?

LIZ. Arnie, stop.

SCOTT. For one thing, I've *tripled* "Slumbertown's" profits.

ARNIE. Sure, by ripping off Calvin Klein and Ralph Lauren.

SCOTT. (*Correcting Arnie.*) *Lauren*, Arnie. And that's better than ripping off Little Orphan Annie!

STEPHANIE. That's enough, Scott.

SCOTT. He started it. Oh, and one other thing, I *did* graduate from a fairly challenging University, *Princeton.* How about you? Wasn't it one semester at some community college?

ARNIE. *Yeah,* 'cause that's all I *needed*! And didn't you major in architecture and then wimp out and take a cushy job in Daddy's shmatah business?

SCOTT. You've got nerve calling *me* a wimp? At least I support my family, all by myself, without my wife's help.

HONEY. (*Angrily, stepping between them.*) Goddamit! Now stop it, both of you!

ARNIE. I'm sorry, Honey. (*HE tosses the tee shirt to Scott.*) *Here,* give this to someone who needs it! And if you want to discuss this further, you know where to find me. (*ARNIE exits.*)

SCOTT. And you know where to find me!

ARNIE. (*O.S.*) *And you know where to find me!*

(*We see JUNIOR'S hand wave a white hanky from the bedroom door. Then HE enters.*)

JUNIOR. Has a truce been called yet?

HONEY. It's just a little flareup.

LIZ. (*Pointing O.S. angrily.*) Daddy, you've been *smoking* in there!

JUNIOR. I've been *leaking* in there.

LIZ. Honey, am I allowed to call him on this?

HONEY. I'll do it. (*To Junior.*) You're not fooling anyone. There's smoke coming out of that bathroom. (*SHE points O.S.*)

JUNIOR. You're right. I'd better see my urologist. Where's Arnie?

LIZ. He went back to our cabin to work.

SCOTT. Which reminds me, I promised to call Bloomingdale's today. And it's almost noon in New York. Excuse me. (*HE checks watch, starts to exit.*)

STEPHANIE. Scott?!

SCOTT. Yes, darling?

STEPHANIE. You just talked to Bloomingdale's on Thursday.

SCOTT. That's right. And they asked me to call back today, which means, I get more orders and you get more mink carcasses to wear.

(SCOTT exits with his drink. STEPHANIE pouts.)

HONEY. *(To Junior, changing the subject.)* Well, it's early to bed tonight, my love. Tomorrow we're going to have a wonderful day in St. Petersburg.

JUNIOR. Y'know, I've been thinking about that, I don't think I'll go.

HONEY. *(Controlling her reaction.)* Why not? Don't you feel well?

JUNIOR. I feel okay. I'm just not thrilled with Russia.

LIZ. Daddy, St. Petersburg isn't that different from St. Louis.

JUNIOR. It's a lot different if I need a doctor. What the hell do Russians know about modern medicine? They can't even make a decent sportcoat.

HONEY. You're not going to need a doctor. But for your information, I checked and there are excellent hospitals in St. Petersburg. Their doctors speak English and they're as good as ours.

STEPHANIE. Daddy, you can't miss the Hermitage. It's the most important museum in the world.

JUNIOR. *Ehh,* I hear it smells like Bolshevik armpits. Honey, you go to St. Petersburg without me. I'll be fine here.

HONEY. *(With a great deal of control.)* If you really don't want to go, I'll stay here with you.

LIZ. *Mother!?* You know how much you've been looking forward to The Hermitage. You studied it for a year. (*SHE turns to Junior.*) Daddy, I just have to say something!

HONEY. (*Firmly.*) No you *don't*, Liz.

JUNIOR. Honey's right, angry daughters are her department.

LIZ. I'm not angry. I'm disappointed.

JUNIOR. *My* department is talking to *sons*, as soon as Honey has one. Did I tell you, we're trying to get her biological clock started again. I think shaking her might help. (*Starting to exit.*)

LIZ. Sure, Daddy, just tell a joke and leave. That solves everything.

JUNIOR. Right, as long as you make sure you *back* out of the room. (*Backing out, to Honey.*) I'll be in the card room, separating old farts from their money.

(*JUNIOR exits. LIZ, lets out a loud grunt, her way of venting frustration.*)

HONEY. I appreciate your self control, Liz.

LIZ. I've got to get out of here. (*SHE starts to exit.*)

STEPHANIE. Liz, don't leave!

LIZ. Why not? Nobody wants to hear the truth. I'm tired of keeping everything in here. (*SHE points to her stomach.*) In the meantime, I've lost complete respect for my father.

HONEY. (*To Liz.*) That's the last thing you should do.

STEPHANIE. Let's just drop this, before we upset Honey again.

HONEY. No, I want to talk about it. Liz, you should know a little more about your father before you give up on him. Let me show you something. I brought this for Daddy to wear to the masquerade party. (*SHE produces a pullover high school letter sweater with a "U" on the chest.*)

STEPHANIE. Oh, Daddy's high school letter sweater.

HONEY. Three years, first string quarterback for the U City Indians.

LIZ. We all know he was a football star.

HONEY. But you don't know this story. We were going steady in Daddy's senior year, and he took me to a big basketball game, wearing this sweater. As usual, he got angry at a referee.

LIZ. Honey, I'm sure this is amusing but what does it have to do with ...

HONEY. (*Interrupting, gently but insistently.*) Liz, please shut up. Just for a minute. I'm doing this the best way I know how.

LIZ. I'm sorry. Go ahead.

HONEY. (*Displaying the sweater to the girls.*) So, to let the referee know how he felt, Daddy gathered up three football player friends of his from different high schools. They were all wearing their letter sweaters and he lined them up. First, a boy from Ferguson, with his "F," then Daddy, with his "U," then a boy from Clayton and then one from Kirkwood.

STEPHANIE. (*Enjoying it, along with Honey.*) One from *Kirkwood.*

HONEY. And they just stood in front of the poor man, *growling.*

STEPHANIE. (*Amused.*) That's my father.

HONEY. We all got kicked out. I was furious.

LIZ. And that's why I should have respect for Daddy?

HONEY. No Liz, it's what happened after that. We got in a big fight that night. And that weekend Martin Berger called and asked me out. I was so angry at Junior, I said yes. Besides, Martin was handsome and exciting.

STEPHANIE. And he probably had hair then.

HONEY. Daddy was so jealous. He came to my house on Westminster and told me to cancel the date or he'd cancel Martin Berger. I said, "I'll see anyone I wish to." I remember Junior's face. He was so hurt. But neither of us would back down. When he left, we were both crying. A week later is when I had my accident.

STEPHANIE. Oh my God! Is that when it happened?

HONEY. (*SHE nods.*) On a Saturday night, two in the morning. Martin was driving me home from a party, and suddenly a car pulled out of a driveway. Martin couldn't swerve or stop. We smashed head-on into the car.

LIZ. (*Pained and angry.*) *Oh!* And I'll just *bet* Martin was drinking.

HONEY. Yes, I'm afraid he was.

STEPHANIE. You can't get him, Liz. Martin died last year.

HONEY. I went right through the windshield. That's what they told me. I don't remember a thing. I was on the critical list for two weeks, unconscious most of the time. For awhile they thought I'd lose the sight in both of my eyes. Thank God it was only in one.

STEPHANIE. You were seventeen.

HONEY. Sixteen. Whenever I woke up, there was this warm hand gripping mine. That was your father, Liz. He never left my side. I found out later that he slept at the foot of my bed every night, till I was out of danger. He kept telling me he loved me more than ever.

STEPHANIE. (*Very moved.*) Oh.

HONEY. And I thought, he's only saying that out of loyalty. He couldn't love me. I looked just awful, all bruised and swollen. But ... he kept squeezing my hand, until ... I finally believed him. Junior gave me the strength I needed. And he's always been my protector. But now Liz, I'm protecting him. And he can't handle that, so he jokes about it. That's our code. He's just saying, "Can you help me, Honey?" It'll take awhile Liz, but he'll be himself again.

LIZ. Okay, I'm off your back about Daddy forever.

HONEY. (*Dryly.*) Can I get that in writing? (*SHE rises, picks up an envelope.*) I'd better turn my Hermitage tickets back to the Tour Director. Could you wait here, in case Daddy comes back?

LIZ. Sure but just return *one* ticket. I'll go into St. Petersburg in the morning and come back and be with Daddy while you go in.

STEPHANIE. Me too.

HONEY. That's sweet, girls, but I wouldn't hear of it.

LIZ. *Honey*, you are going to the Hermitage, or we're both going to hold our breath.

(*LIZ and STEPHANIE look at each other, nod, take a deep breath and hold it.*)

HONEY. All right, if you promise Daddy won't hear one word about cholesterol or sex.

STEPHANIE. We promise.

(HONEY reacts and exits. STEPHANIE calls O.S.)

STEPHANIE. But for your information, sex lowers cholesterol. (*Looking at a map, to Liz.*) Okay, we'll catch the nine o'clock bus in and then ...

LIZ. Go ahead, Steph, let me have it. Boy, do I deserve it.

STEPHANIE. What do you mean?

LIZ. My little tantrum over your mink. I was a real horse's ass!

STEPHANIE. But that's *you*, Liz. I mean I should have remembered how tight you are with your furry little friends.

LIZ. But I'm tighter with my sister, for God's sake. Forgive me, I'm just off on a tangent lately, trying to deal with Arnie.

STEPHANIE. What's wrong?

LIZ. Where do I begin? You won't tell Scott?

STEPHANIE. I tell Scott nothing.

LIZ. Well, Arnie's kind of depressed about his writing career. It could be going a lot better.

STEPHANIE. *That's* why you haven't told him about your new job?

LIZ. Yeah. And lately, he thinks the answer to his depression is having sex.

STEPHANIE. *Often?*

LIZ. If sex alone built self-esteem, Arnie would be an egomaniac. And the more he wants it, the more frustrated I get.

STEPHANIE. Liz, I'm really trying to sympathize with you, *honest.* But Scott and I make love about once every two or three weeks. And then it's only because we're making up.

LIZ. God, it's like we're all part of a Russian play. A mother and her two daughters and the three men who are driving them insane. (*SHE holds the jacket for Stephanie trying to hide her repugnance.*) Here, try this on. Actually it's very pretty. Wear it ... in good health. And remember, no matter how mean and vicious I might get, I *love* my sister.

STEPHANIE. Too bad you don't *respect* your sister.

LIZ. That's not true. I respect plenty about you. You're smart, you're talented, you're fun to be with. You have great taste.

STEPHANIE. It sounds like you're rushing me for a sorority.

LIZ. Like hell, these are things I envy. You're a born leader. I've always told you how much I admire your confidence.

STEPHANIE. You've always told me I'm a know-it-all.

LIZ. That's what I meant. And you were the best Hunger Drive chairman ever. Even better than *me*. (*A tough admission.*) Everyone said so. And of course, if we're talking total respect, I never forget ... your *boobs*. (*SHE stares at Stephanie's chest.*)

STEPHANIE. (*Gloating.*) Right, it's the one thing Honey didn't divide fair and equal.

LIZ. Every time I put on a padded bra, I hate you.

STEPHANIE. I count on that.

LIZ. Really Steph, you have terrific potential.

STEPHANIE. Which I'm not using?

LIZ. Not nearly enough. But you could, if you'd stop driving yourself crazy trying to get Scott's approval.

STEPHANIE. Which I never get anyway.

LIZ. Steph, I don't think there's *anything* you can't do.

STEPHANIE. You're right, dammit. (*STEPHANIE rises, with the mink jacket.*)

LIZ. Where are you going?

STEPHANIE. To return this.

LIZ. (*SHE rises.*) Stephanie, that's *wonderful*.

STEPHANIE. Yeah, it shows real character. (*As STEPHANIE exits.*) This better earn me some respect from you, *bitch*.

LIZ. *Total*. (*LIZ smiles.*)

(*LIGHTS CROSSFADE to Liz's room. ARNIE is typing. We hear BELL TONES.*)

FEMALE INTOURIST GUIDE. (*Russian accent.*) Good afternoon ladies and gentlemen. This is your Intourist guide, Ludmilla. We hope you are enjoying our sunny day in St. Petersburg. The afternoon tour of the Hermitage Museum is now meeting at the red tour bus.

LIZ. (*Enters wearing a red Russian tee shirt.*) Here you are. I can't believe you giving Scott the silent treatment at lunch.

ARNIE. It wasn't the silent treatment, it's a language barrier. I don't speak "Asshole."

LIZ. Steph was impressed that I found something wearable to buy in Russia. Here, I got you a Russian chocolate bar.

ARNIE. No thanks.

LIZ. No thanks? You're *writing*? Your *"Mugsy?"*

ARNIE. No, my mommy and daddy.

LIZ. Oh? Send them my love?

ARNIE. (*HE hands her the paper.*) I did. Here, you'd better read this. In case you have any comments.

LIZ. (*SHE reads, then angrily.*) I'll *kill* you! Arnie we're not moving back to St. Louis because of Scott's stupid insults! I can't believe that you see insects as your life's work!

ARNIE. I *don't.* I see a seventy thousand a year as my life's work. Dad says that's the floor, plus a bonus if termites are bad again this year. Why the hell are you making me apologize for supporting my family?

LIZ. Because, you can do it as a writer, if you don't give up.

ARNIE. You don't want me to give up, huh? You must really believe in my talent.

LIZ. Of course I do.

ARNIE. It wouldn't have to do with anything else would it?

LIZ. What do you mean? Like what?

ARNIE. Like Mickey Fucking Mouse? Walt Disney? Your new job?

LIZ. How did you find out?

ARNIE. They called last week for your social security number. Nothing gets by us house husbands. I've been waiting a week for you to tell me. Why didn't you?

LIZ. I wanted to, the minute after I got the job, but I was afraid it would depress you. That was the day your agent wasn't returning your phone calls.

ARNIE. So why didn't you tell me the next day?

LIZ. That was the day your agent dropped you. Then I decided to wait till we were on the trip, when you'd be in an "up" mood. *Ha!* Well now you know. What do you think?

ARNIE. It sounds like a great job. I'm sorry you won't be able to take it.

LIZ. Why not? We love California, you love writing. There'll be more money, so you can write what you want to write. We can even think about buying a house. It's a wonderful opportunity.

ARNIE. For *you.*

LIZ. Not just for me, for both of us. Don't you see? And what's wrong with it being wonderful for *me*?

ARNIE. Nothing, if you were married to somebody else. Liz, what did you expect, that I'd just gracefully let you take over the support of our family? I make a lousy gigolo.

LIZ. Arnie, I realize something now. You know why I didn't tell you about my job right away? I was afraid your male image might be more important to you than my happiness. Guess what? I was right.

ARNIE. It won't work, Babe. I'm guilt-proof on this one.

LIZ. No really, suddenly I'm discovering a lot about us. Our marriage is solid as a rock, as long I walk four steps behind you. But if I get a little success before you do, we're in big trouble.

ARNIE. (*HE takes the letter, starts to exit.*) I've got to mail this. It's a decision I had to make.

LIZ. And I guess I'll have to make *my* own decision too?

ARNIE. (*Making an important point.*) I love you. (*ARNIE exits.*)

(*LIGHTS CROSSFADE to Stephanie's room. STEPHANIE hides behind the door, wearing mink earmuffs as SCOTT enters. He's going to jog on the deck.*)

STEPHANIE. Hi, I was looking for your passport and guess what I found? (*SHE adjusts the earmuffs.*)

SCOTT. Oh, the mink earmuffs?

STEPHANIE. They're beautiful. Now I'm even happier that I took my jacket back. Because these were *your* idea. When were you going to give them to me?

SCOTT. (*Trying to get past a sticky situation.*) Hmmm. Well, to tell the truth, they're a little business gift for Marci. It's her birthday. But keep 'em if you want. I'll get her another pair.

STEPHANIE. (*Totally deflated.*) You shithead! Why couldn't you have just lied and said they were for me? (*SHE exits with the earmuffs.*)

SCOTT. (*Jokingly, exiting after her.*) Listen Steph ... I got you these earmuffs.

(*WE hear the sound of a TOILET FLUSH.*)

SCOTT. (*O.S. Upset.*) Not in the *toilet*!

(*STEPHANIE enters, followed by SCOTT carrying dripping earmuffs which HE drops in waste can.*)

STEPHANIE. And I suppose you're going to stick with your story that your relationship with Marci is all business?

SCOTT. I never said it was all business. But it isn't sex, it's friendship. We have lunch, maybe catch a show. That's all.

STEPHANIE. And I'm supposed to accept all this because you said she's fat and unattractive.

SCOTT. Forget I ever mentioned that.

STEPHANIE. I knew it, she's beautiful, isn't she?

SCOTT. No, she's fat and unattractive, but it was cruel of me to say that. The important thing is, Marci is bright and funny and interesting to talk to.

STEPHANIE. Oh? And you desperately need these things, because you don't get them at home?

SCOTT. I've never said that. But it is nice to talk to a woman who has more on her mind than "What's Cher gonna wear to the Oscars?"

STEPHANIE. You know that's not all I talk about. *If* I can find someone to communicate with.

SCOTT. Oh oh, you're using "communicate." We're in trouble.

STEPHANIE. For your information, I read a lot more than you do. And probably more than *Marci* too. And I'd be glad to match I.Q. scores with either of you.

SCOTT. I wouldn't make this a contest if I were you. Marci graduated with honors from Stanford. Where did you go? The University of Shopping? Rah! And didn't you come home crying after three weeks?

STEPHANIE. You son of a bitch. Westbury College for Women is a damn good school. It's only two blocks from Harvard. And I only came home because I was confused and homesick. If you had any respect for me, you'd understand that.

SCOTT. Stephanie, I'll give you anything money can buy. But respect's a little different. *That* you've got to earn. I'm gonna take a run. (*HE grabs sweat clothes from under his bed.*)

STEPHANIE. You're not running right now. I want to discuss this. (*SHE grabs his jockstrap.*)

SCOTT. (*Holding his hand out.*) All right, hand over my jockstrap!

STEPHANIE. Your balls can *flap in the wind* for all I care! I want to talk about our marriage.

SCOTT. (*Lightly.*) Big mistake. Y'see, I treat our marriage like a litter box. If you don't dig too deep, you won't find the shit. (*HE grabs the jockstrap from her and exits to the bathroom.*)

STEPHANIE. (*Calling O.S.*) Very funny Scott. How funny do you think *this* is. Maybe we should think about divorce.

SCOTT (*O.S. Chuckling.*) We can't get a divorce. We're unbeatable at mixed doubles.

STEPHANIE. Goddamit, you better take me seriously. (*HE enters wearing his sweatpants, pulling on his sweatshirt.*)

SCOTT. Just stop throwing words around, okay? I don't want a divorce. Besides, you're not going out there alone and you know it. You can't even spend a whole cocktail party at the other end of the room. (*Making a sincere effort.*) All right, you want to talk? I'm listening. (*HE sits, ties his shoes.*)

STEPHANIE. I spent last night thinking about what Daddy did when Honey had her accident.

SCOTT. That thing you told me about him sleeping at the foot of her hospital bed?

STEPHANIE. Yes. And the way they've always been so much in love, and the way they laugh together. Scott, I don't like feeling envious of my own parents. Be honest, would you ever sleep at the foot of *my* bed?

SCOTT. I don't believe you're putting me through this.

STEPHANIE. You're right, it's silly to compare their marriage with ours. You never even tell me you love me, unless I ask if you do.

SCOTT. (*Long   suffering.*) Oh boy, are we *communicating.*

STEPHANIE. I've also been wondering if I could be as devoted as Honey is, if *you* had a heart attack.

SCOTT. Well, I'd better stay healthy then. (*HE rises.*) Where's my pulse timer? Ah, here we go. (*HE finds the timer-watch, puts it on.*) I shouldn't be gone more than an hour.

STEPHANIE. Scott, don't leave!

SCOTT. I'm *leaving.* What are you gonna do, go home to your mother's state room? (*SCOTT exits.*)

STEPHANIE. (*Calling after him.*) I really don't like you.

(*LIGHTS CROSSFADE to Honey's room. HONEY enters, wearing casual clothes and Reeboks, loading things into a "fanny pack." We hear the THREE BELL TONES.*)

FEMALE INTOURIST GUIDE. (*Russian accent.*) This is the last call for the Hermitage Museum afternoon tour. All passengers with tour tickets will report to the red bus, departing in ten minutes. Thank you.

HONEY. (*Calling O.S.*) I'll be back as soon as I can. All your pills ... are you listening to me?

JUNIOR. (*O.S.*) My hearing aid's in there. Just talk right into it. (*HE enters.*) Go ahead.

HONEY. (*Pointing at the lined up stuff.*) All your pills are here. Why not take your aspirin now? (*SHE hands him water and aspirin, HE takes it.*) Here's your oxygen tank, but you're not going to need it. And here's Sardinehead's number. You won't need that either. Here are the girls' numbers and they'll be dropping by to see you. I'll be back before you know it.

(*The TELEPHONE rings. LIGHTS COME UP in Stephanie's room, SHE is on the phone. We see both sides of the conversation.*)

JUNIOR. (*HE picks up the phone.*) Ingmar's Bar.

STEPHANIE. (*Tearfully.*) Daddy?

JUNIOR. Stephanie? What's wrong? Are you okay?

STEPHANIE. *No.* Can I come up and talk to you?

JUNIOR. (*Apprehensively.*) You want to talk? What about?

STEPHANIE. My awful marriage. I'm divorcing Scott!

JUNIOR. *Jesus*! This is definitely your mother's department.

(*HE starts to hand the phone to Honey, but STEPHANIE shouts.*)

STEPHANIE. *DADDY*! I have to talk to *you*. Can I come up or not?

JUNIOR. (*Into the phone.*) Sure, but give me a few minutes before you do. Bye.

(STEPHANIE and JUNIOR hang up. The LIGHTS DIM in Stephanie's room.)

HONEY. What's wrong?

JUNIOR. I'm in deep shit. Stephanie says she's divorcing Scott.

HONEY. My God, what did he do?

JUNIOR. (*Panicked.*) Who the hell knows? The problem is she wants to talk to *me* about it. And she's crying. Obviously you can't go to St. Petersburg.

HONEY. I suppose you're right.

JUNIOR. Of course I'm right. This emotional stuff's always been your department.

HONEY. But she asked specifically to talk to *you*.

JUNIOR. Just tell her I'm not feeling well and had to lay down for awhile. And you won't be lying. (*HE moves slowly toward bedroom.*)

HONEY. But Darling ...

JUNIOR. I'm not up to this. You know that.

HONEY. Well, okay, if you really feel that shaky.

JUNIOR. I do. Let's not push my luck. You'll say just the right things. You always do. (*HE exits.*)

HONEY. (*SHE thinks, makes a decision.*) Junior. Come back here.

JUNIOR. (*HE reappears at the door.*) What?

HONEY. I can't take you off the hook this time. You're going to have to talk to Stephanie yourself.

JUNIOR. *No*! She's *crying*. You know how that upsets me.

HONEY. So, you'll be upset with the rest of us. For three months I've let you avoid anything you didn't want to do. Which is pretty much *everything*. I can't do that this time. I'm not going to protect you from your own daughter.

JUNIOR. You picked a funny time to get *strict*. You want me to have another heart attack?

HONEY. You're not going to have another heart attack.

JUNIOR. Well I'm not staying around to find out.

(HE moves to exit. SHE blocks his way.)

HONEY. The hell you aren't! You're going to wait for your daughter! Now sit down.

JUNIOR. No.

HONEY. (*SHE takes off her fanny pack and brandishes it like a weapon.*) I'm warning you, *this is a very heavy fanny pack*!

JUNIOR. (*HE sits.*) All right I'll sit down. But in case you're interested, there's definite pain going on in here. (*HE points to his chest.*)

HONEY. Then take a nitro.

(SHE throws him the bottle, HE catches it, puts it down.)

JUNIOR. No, the hell with it! I hope I *do* have another heart attack. I'm a useless bastard and you know it!

HONEY. All I know is you're acting like a spoiled brat instead of the head of your family.

JUNIOR. Well you won't have to put up with me much longer. (*HE takes out the pink capsule and stands up.*)

HONEY. Now what the hell's that?

JUNIOR. This happens to be a "terminator pill."

HONEY. A terminator pill?

JUNIOR. Yes. I made Rubin give it to me, so that when the time came to put an end to my miserable existence, I could make a quick and graceful exit.

HONEY. I see.

JUNIOR. You don't think I'd use it?

HONEY. Who cares? If you're so intent on leaving me forever, I can't stop you. But there is one thing you should know before you take that pill.

JUNIOR. What?

HONEY. It happens to be a *laxative* capsule.

JUNIOR. You're out of your mind!

HONEY. Am I? Why don't you call Rubin? He told me all about the "terminator." He said you asked for "a quick way to go." And that's exactly what you've got there.

JUNIOR. That son of a bitch! Okay, I'll find another way to do it. And believe me, you'll be a lot better off.

HONEY. *Damn you,* will you stop these stupid suicide threats?! You'd find a way to wiggle out of something you didn't want to do, even if it killed you! Well not this time, I'm calling your bluff. Your manipulating days are over!

JUNIOR. Who's trying to manipulate anyone?

HONEY. *You* are! You always have. What do you call it when you're too tired to dance one dance, but you'll stand up all day in a fishing canoe in a freezing downpour? And what do you call it when you're too weak to walk up two steps but you'll work for hours in your garden pushing a wheelbarrow full of fertilizer?

JUNIOR. I'd call that horseshit.

HONEY. Liz is right. You never fail to have a funny answer. What's your funny answer for not being a father when your daughters were growing up?

JUNIOR. I resent that. I was always there, right behind you. Is it my fault I don't know how to lead a Girl Scout troop? What did you want me to do, talk them through their first period?

HONEY. *Yes,* if that's what they needed from you! (*Putting on her fanny pack.*) Now, *I* am leaving to go into The Hermitage. And *you* are going to face your daughter and talk to her. Unless you want to take the easy way out and kill yourself. There's enough nitroglycerine pills there to do the job. And if that doesn't work, *swallow your oxygen tank for all I care!* (*HONEY opens the door and exits.*)

STEPHANIE. (*Enters, looks back at Honey.*) Goodbye, Honey. (*Apologetically, to Junior.*) Is this a bad time?

JUNIOR. We'll find out, won't we? Come on in. So, you're having a problem?

STEPHANIE. Yes, and I'm going to get rid of him. But I want to discuss something more important. You and me.

JUNIOR. (*HE reacts and sits.*) You and me? Okay. (*HE takes a nitro out, just in case.*) I don't know how good I'll be at this. We haven't had that many father/daughter talks.

STEPHANIE. We've *never* had a father/daughter talk.

JUNIOR. Of course we have. We used to talk a lot when we did all those fun things together, like riding and going to baseball games. And we had plenty of talks when I taught you how to play poker.

STEPHANIE. Daddy, your saying, "Never smile when you get a full house," doesn't count as a talk.

JUNIOR. Well we're going to have one now. Just be patient with me if I say something stupid.

STEPHANIE. Don't worry, I will.

JUNIOR. All right, let's talk about your marriage. I always like to bring up the positives first. What do we have here? For one thing, Scott is a good provider.

(SHE begins whimpering. HE reacts.)

JUNIOR. I think I said something stupid. Why don't you talk first?

STEPHANIE. For fifteen years, Scott's been making me feel like a beautiful appendage, the most expensive baby sitter in the world.

JUNIOR. That's awful. And he's totally wrong, Steph. You're a fine talented girl.

STEPHANIE. Daddy, I'm thirty-six. And I'm trying to be honest with myself. Scott doesn't love me. Not the way you love Honey. Not even the way he loves "Slumbertown." And the truth is I don't love him either.

JUNIOR. Does he know you're thinking about divorce?

STEPHANIE. Yes. He just laughed and said I'd never divorce him. I'd be too terrified to be out there alone. He's right. I am scared. And Daddy, it's your fault.

JUNIOR. My fault? That sounds familiar. You want to explain that? (*HE takes a nitro, holds his heart.*)

STEPHANIE. Oh God, you're doing your Napoleon. This is too much stress for you. (*Moving to the door.*)

JUNIOR. It is *not*. Go on. (*HE takes the nitro out of his mouth, throws it across the room.*)

STEPHANIE. No Daddy, I'm being selfish. We'll talk sometime in St. Louis.

JUNIOR. I already wasted a pill. I want to talk *now*!

STEPHANIE. We've talked enough. You're a sick man.

JUNIOR. (*Definitely in charge.*) I'm not a sick man, I'm your father. And when I say we're going to talk, *we're going to talk*! You don't tell a guy he's a lousy father and then walk out the door.

STEPHANIE. Daddy, you're not a lousy father. You're *wonderful*. I wouldn't trade you for any other father in the world. (*SHE returns to face him.*)

JUNIOR. Good, I'm off the trading block. (*HE holds his heart, then stops.*) Now, why is your unhappiness my fault?

STEPHANIE. I know how much you wanted a son, Stephen Frank the Third, to bring into the family business and teach football to. And then I was born, all you got was the name. Stephanie.

JUNIOR. Now I'm not gonna lie and say I didn't want a son. I was afraid a daughter might end up with this face. (*HE points to his face.*) But you know I'm nuts about you. As far as I'm concerned, you can't do anything wrong.

STEPHANIE. See, that's how you screwed me up! You were always too easy on me. And when I became a teenager, you just turned me over to Honey.

JUNIOR. But you were a young lady. What could I have said to you?

STEPHANIE. If I had been your son, you would have had plenty to say. And demanded much more.

JUNIOR. I don't know about that.

(HE moves away, SHE stays in pursuit.)

STEPHANIE. I do. Remember when I entered college. And I called after a week and said I hated it and I begged you to let me come home. What did you do?

JUNIOR. I let you come home. But there were extenuating circumstances.

STEPHANIE. What?

JUNIOR. You were crying!

STEPHANIE. If I were your son, what would you have done?

JUNIOR. *Jesus!* I didn't know this was going to be questions and answers. I guess if you were my son, I would have done what my father did when I dropped out of college. Hell yes, I'd have taken you into the business and started you from the ground up and, *boy,* made you work your ass off.

STEPHANIE. I accept.

JUNIOR. What?

STEPHANIE. What's good enough for your son, is good enough for me.

JUNIOR. Very funny.

STEPHANIE. I'm not kidding, Daddy. I need a job. I've never needed anything so much in my life.

JUNIOR. But I'm in the pants business.

STEPHANIE. That's my specialty, knowing what looks good in pants.

JUNIOR. But I've already told you, I'm selling the business.

STEPHANIE. I know. You can tell United Textiles I'm part of the package. If there's one thing I'm good at, it's style. Remember in the Sixties, when you made those Nehru jackets? *I'm* the one who told you you'd be stuck with 'em.

JUNIOR. (*A painful memory.*) Yeah, I remember. We sold a *few*.

STEPHANIE. Daddy, I can help bring Frank Brothers into the Twenty-first Century.

JUNIOR. Stephanie, this is crazy. I know you're feeling lousy about your marriage but going to work for Frank Brothers isn't the answer. If you're worried about money, you know I'm going to back you up. And I'm not gonna let Scott shirk his obligations.

STEPHANIE. I don't want to be an obligation. I want a career!

JUNIOR. Well, open a boutique or go into decorating. You're gifted at that. Don't think you can just walk into a complicated business like mine. You don't know a damn thing about it.

STEPHANIE. That's what you're going to teach me, while you're working my ass off, like you would a son. Daddy, I'm a salesman. You think it's easy to sell a thousand dollar ad in a hunger drive magazine to a builder who's having a lousy year? If I can sell a hundred thousand dollars worth of those ads, I can sell pants.

JUNIOR. Yeah, I guess you could. But what the hell am I going to do if you don't work out? How am I going to fire my own daughter?

STEPHANIE. You won't have to. I'll put a pink slip in an envelope on your desk, the day I go to work. All you have to do is mail it.—And I'll go to work for your competition.

JUNIOR. It must be hereditary. I threatened Grandpa with that too. Well, at least you won't have to punch out the loading dock foreman to prove yourself, like *I* did. She was a *tough* old broad.—All right, let me talk this over with your mother.

STEPHANIE. No you don't! Not *this* time. This is *your* department.

JUNIOR. You don't let *up*.

STEPHANIE. That's right. Do I have a job?

JUNIOR. I guess a daughter's got a right to expect nepotism too. Okay, you've got a job, Kiddo. *(HE shakes her hand.)*

STEPHANIE. Daddy, I know I'm asking a lot. Thanks. *(SHE hugs Junior.)*

JUNIOR. Don't thank me, just go after my job. Hey, this might be fun. Tell you what, we get back Saturday. I'll pick you up Monday morning and we'll drive down to the office together.

STEPHANIE. Terrific. You sure Monday's okay for you, with jet lag and everything?

JUNIOR. Just worry about yourself daughter. And I get to work *early*. Be ready at eight sharp.

STEPHANIE. I'll be at the curb. But make it 7:30, so you can show me around the factory before work.

JUNIOR. Jesus. I may be facing an internal takeover.

STEPHANIE. Okay, I've worn you out enough. You get some rest. (*SHE kisses him, starts to leave.*)

JUNIOR. Hold on a minute. I'm not tired. And there's one other thing I'd like to get straight here.

STEPHANIE. Yeah?

JUNIOR. What we had just now, that was a goddam talk, right?!

STEPHANIE. Yes, Daddy. That was a goddam talk.

JUNIOR. (*Grinning, on a high.*) *Goddam* it, that was *fun*!

(*THEY exit together. LIGHTS UP on Liz's room. ARNIE enters, followed by SCOTT, whose Princeton tee shirt is soaked with sweat.*)

ARNIE (*O.S.*) Scott? What are you doing here?

SCOTT. (*O.S.*) I'd like to to talk to you, Arn.

ARNIE. What happened, d'ya fall overboard?

SCOTT. I was running.

ARNIE. Look, I don't want to fight.

SCOTT. Neither do I. Sorry, I was a little rough on you yesterday.

ARNIE. That's okay. I was rough too.

SCOTT. We're the outsiders in this family. We've got to stick together. Besides, I'm not ready to lose you as a friend.

ARNIE. *We're friends*?

SCOTT. I've always thought so. Are you saying we're not?

ARNIE. No, I'm not saying that.

SCOTT. Good. Clean slate, guy? (*HE offers his hand, Ivy League style.*)

ARNIE. Sure, guy.

(THEY shake hands, then SCOTT hugs Arnie.)

SCOTT. Arn, I need your help.

ARNIE. (*Dealing with his now damp shirt.*) Yeah?

SCOTT. Stephanie and I just had a little ... blood letting. Slightly worse than the usual. So, I'm running around the Promenade Deck, thinking, I do not have a good marriage.

ARNIE. Okay.

SCOTT. And at the same time I'm thinking, Liz and Arnie *do* have a good marriage. Why?

ARNIE. I don't know, for one thing, we both *think* we do.

SCOTT. That's good, that's positive thinking. Maybe you and Liz could talk to Stephanie for me?

ARNIE. You want us to convince her you're a great husband?

SCOTT. No, just that I'm trying. She doesn't think I try, which is total bullshit. I have never said no to her, regardless of what she wants. Does that sound like I'm a guy who doesn't care?

ARNIE. Scott, you *do* want to stay married?

SCOTT. Of course. Divorce is one complication I *don't* need.

ARNIE. Well I figure if a marriage is gonna work, it's got to have three things.

SCOTT. Yeah? What?

ARNIE. Love, respect and laughs.

SCOTT. (*HE considers it for a beat.*) Those formula things don't work for me. Not that I don't try that stuff. But Stephanie's a bottomless pit. She's got to be reassured constantly, about everything.

ARNIE. Do you love her?

SCOTT. Have you been talking to *her*? That's all *she* wants to know. Of course I love her. I'm proud as hell when I walk into a room with Stephanie. But I also have other things to worry about. Like a business that doesn't move an inch if I don't push it. And believe me, there are plenty of people who'd love to see me fall on my ass.

ARNIE. I'll bet.

SCOTT. Why am I always supposed to be understanding with *her*? When's she gonna start trying to understand *me*? Shit, y'know I think what Freud said on his death bed was right.

ARNIE. (*Dryly.*) Oh, you mean, "Cancel that strudel?"

SCOTT. Sorry, I wasn't throwing Princeton at you.

ARNIE. No, go ahead, throw it.

SCOTT. Listen, with all my psych courses, you're happier than I am.

ARNIE. Hey, now you got me curious. What did "Siggy" say?

SCOTT. What Freud said was, "*What do women want?*"

LIZ. (*Enters.*) Hi.

ARNIE. Hi.

SCOTT. Hi, Liz. I'd better see if Stephanie's back. Thanks, guy. (*SCOTT exits.*)

ARNIE. Sure, guy. (*To Liz.*) Where were you?

LIZ. Trying to find *you* ... to tell you something. If it means that much to you, we'll go back to St. Louis.

ARNIE. You wouldn't mind?

LIZ. I'd mind, but I'd go.

ARNIE. What about your job at Disney?

LIZ. It's not as important to me as you are.

ARNIE. But they told me you'd have your own office and your own parking space on "Goofy Drive."

LIZ. I know. You still come out ahead. *Barely.* I'll find a good company in St. Louis. But Arnie, I happen to be excellent at what I do. If I end up as President of Ralston Purina, are you gonna be able to deal with that?

ARNIE. *No.*—Because we're not going back to St. Louis. I didn't send the letter.

LIZ. Why not?

ARNIE. Let me tell you something about the males in my family. I'm a jerk, my father's a jerk, my grandfather was a jerk. No, he was a shmuck. I come from a tradition of big pride, big ego and big balls. I can't change myself, but I love your ass. So I'm gonna lay down on the tracks for you. I might get up and run before the train comes.—I want you to take the Disney job.

LIZ. Thanks.

ARNIE. So, you'll be making twice as much as I do.

LIZ. *Three* times.

ARNIE. *Jesus.* Y'know now that I've bought the idea, *three* times is a lot easier to take. Congratulations, I'm proud of you.

LIZ. I'm proud of you too.

(THEY kiss.)

ARNIE. You better be. I'm feeling okay about myself, after my talk with Scott. It's funny, I have a whole different attitude about that guy.

LIZ. You mean you don't want him dead anymore?

ARNIE. Not for the time being. He's really pathetic and *lost*. He's got a terrific girl like Stephanie and he doesn't love her. He doesn't know how to love. You know, he'd never admit it, but he envies us plenty. Even if he does think you're cheap and I'm tasteless.

LIZ. A good marriage is the best revenge.

ARNIE. You're goddam right.

LIZ. (*SHE hugs him.*) I'm so excited about my new job. Now I can afford to do something I've been thinking about for the longest time.

ARNIE. You mean adding a hard disk to your Macintosh?

LIZ. No, I want bigger boobs.

ARNIE. (*Shocked.*) *What*?!

LIZ. A breast enhancement operation, so I feel better in my new clothes. And I'm sure you wouldn't mind it.

ARNIE. Are you kidding me?

LIZ. It's simple. They make a little slit right here and put in a silicone pouch.

ARNIE. (*Squirming in imagined pain.*) *Ahhh!* Don't even joke about doing that. Are you crazy? Silly Putty tits?

LIZ. It's not dangerous.

ARNIE. How do you know? Haven't you been reading all that stuff about implants? They don't know the long term effects of that shit. I'm not letting you roll the dice with your life.

LIZ. But your eyes are always on Stephanie's cleavage.

ARNIE. Hey, I'm fascinated by the San Andreas Fault, but I don't want to sleep with it.

LIZ. You honestly feel that way?

ARNIE. Absolutely. Haven't I ever told you? I hate big tits. I'm hooked on the smell of foam rubber. (*HE buries his face in her chest.*)

(*The LIGHTS BLACKOUT, then FADE UP in Stephanie's room. We hear THREE BELL TONES. STEPHANIE is on the bed.*)

CAPTAIN'S VOICE. (*SPEAKER.*) This is Captain Nordenkjell. Tonight, a real treat aboard the Royal Norway. Our staff and crew will do clog dances to Norwegian folk music. And I would like to offer special congratulations to Mr. and Mrs. Stephan Frank Jr. and their happy family, who are celebrating a very important anniversary tonight. Or as we say in Norwegian, Gratolara Miadagen.

SCOTT. (*Enters in running clothes.*) Hi, where you been?

STEPHANIE. Talking with Daddy, in his room. He's offered me a job at Frank Brothers.

SCOTT. (*HE chuckles.*) What really happened? Be serious.

STEPHANIE. I am serious. He's decided not to retire. He's going to take me into Frank Brothers and teach me the whole business, from the stock room up.

SCOTT. That's ridiculous. What good are you gonna be in the mens' clothing business?

STEPHANIE. Daddy seemed excited about having a new Frank in the company. And I think he also feels good about preparing me for my new life ... without *you*.

SCOTT. What the hell are you talking about?

STEPHANIE. I don't love you Scott.

SCOTT. You discussed this with Junior?

STEPHANIE. Of course, he's my father.

SCOTT. You want me to say I love you, right?

STEPHANIE. No.

SCOTT. Well I want to say it. I love you. Okay?

STEPHANIE. You don't have to move out right away. You can sleep in the guest room while you find an apartment.

SCOTT. Look, why didn't you say you wanted to work? You can work for ... with *me,* at "Slumbertown."

STEPHANIE. That's a lousy idea. I'm sure neither of our lawyers would go for that.

SCOTT. Will you stop this? I apologize. For whatever you're pissed off about, I am really sorry. There, isn't that what you want?

STEPHANIE. I just told you what I want.

SCOTT. You're *not* getting a divorce. I don't want a divorce. You're very important to me. And to Donny and Rick. What kind of mother would leave her boys when they need her most?

STEPHANIE. I'm not leaving. *You're* leaving. Don't worry, you can have the boys on the weekends, for their "How to be a winner" lessons.

SCOTT. Stephanie, *come on,* I'll never talk to Marci again. I'll dump Bloomingdale's if you want me to.

STEPHANIE. I wouldn't do that. You don't want to lose your best account and your marriage at the same time.

SCOTT. (*An understanding smile.*) Go ahead, Steph, I don't blame you. It's healthy getting these things out, communicating.

STEPHANIE. I'll go up to the ship's store and buy you some dry earmuffs for Marci. (*SHE starts to exit.*)

SCOTT. Wait! *Forget* that! Look for one thing, please don't discuss this with your parents anymore. You don't want to ruin their anniversary party? Now we have plenty of time to make things right between us, starting now. Number one, I'm on Perrier tonight, okay? And two, if that's where you want me, at the foot of your bed, you got it. Of course, I wouldn't mind you being down there with me. See I'll give you what you want. (*HE kneels on the floor.*)

STEPHANIE. Scott, please get up. You can't give me what I want. You know how you've always said I'm spoiled rotten?

SCOTT. Yes, but I said that with a lot of affection.

STEPHANIE. No, you were right, I *am* spoiled, I've been spoiled all my life by the very best. By my parents' wonderful marriage. By living in a house with a man like Daddy. The problem is, I'm just too spoiled to settle for any less. I won't lower my standards anymore to accommodate you, Scott. I don't have to.

SCOTT. Stephanie, I'll change, I promise. Just give me a chance. *Please?*

STEPHANIE. I'm sorry Scott. I'm sure you'd try, or at least, you'd think you were trying; but you're not going to change. (*SHE starts to exit, then stops.*) I never thought it would give me so little pleasure to say this. You lose. (*SHE exits.*)

SCOTT. Stephanie! (*SCOTT exits.*)

(*LIGHTS CROSSFADE to Honey's room. JUNIOR enters, putting on his letter sweater.*)

JUNIOR. (*Sings to tune of "On Wisconsin."*) On U City, On U City, Fight right through that line. (*H E growls.*) Grrrr!

(*There's a KNOCK at the door.*)

LIZ. (*O.S.*) Daddy, hi, it's Liz.
JUNIOR. Come on in.

(*LIZ and ARNIE, noshing from a plate, enter.*)

LIZ. Just checking in to see how you're doing? Oh Daddy, you're wearing your "FUCK sweater."
ARNIE. What?
LIZ. I'll explain later. (*To Daddy.*) Honey left for St. Petersburg?
JUNIOR. Yeah, she uh ... took off.
ARNIE. (*HE offers Junior his plate.*) Junior?
JUNIOR. Thanks, Arnie. (*JUNIOR takes a snack.*) How many smorgasbords does this make for you today?
ARNIE. Just *one* ... but it's continuous.
LIZ. Stephanie told us the wonderful news about your offering her a job and going back to work.
JUNIOR. Is that what I did? (*Then smiling.*) Yeah, Stephie and I are gonna be a team.
HONEY. (*Enters. To Junior.*) Hi. You okay?
JUNIOR. Compared to *who*?
HONEY. (*Reassured.*) You're okay

LIZ. Honey, what are you doing here? Why aren't you at The Hermitage?

HONEY. (*SHE shrugs.*) I heard the place smells like Bolshevik armpits. Liz, could you excuse us? Daddy and I need to talk.

LIZ. Sure. Daddy, I'm so proud of you. (*SHE hugs him emotionally.*)

JUNIOR. Thanks, daughter.

ARNIE. I was *always* proud of you.

JUNIOR. What, no hug?

ARNIE. Hell, yes.

(ARNIE and JUNIOR hug.)

JUNIOR. Gotta hang on to you. Looks like you're the only little bastard left.

(As ARNIE turns, JUNIOR gives him a pat on the behind. ARNIE reacts. HE and LIZ exit.)

ARNIE. (*To Liz as HE exits.*) Now, you wanna tell me what a "fuck sweater" is?

JUNIOR. So how come you didn't go to your museum?

HONEY. Didn't feel like it. Had this fight with my boyfriend. So I decided to just "mellow-out," as Stephanie calls it.

JUNIOR. Oh? You had a few drinks at the bar?

HONEY. You don't know anything about women, do you? All the vodka in Russia couldn't have given me the lift I just got from one little ... (*SHE displays her hands, sits.) Manicure.* But now that you've made me think about it, a vodka/tonic sounds even better.

JUNIOR. *(Moving to the bar with energy.)* I got it. One Archeecharnya with malaria juice, coming up.

HONEY. *What? You're* fixing?

JUNIOR. Yeah, I thought I'd kiss up to you a little, since you had that mishap before, when your head exploded.

HONEY. I'm fine now. I stuffed everything back in.

JUNIOR. You haven't been that angry at me since the last time I wore this sweater.

HONEY. I guess I haven't.

JUNIOR. At least this time, you can't go out with Martin Berger.

HONEY. I wouldn't, even if I could.

JUNIOR. Smart, in his condition, he'd be a dull date.

HONEY. So tell me, what happened with Stephanie?

JUNIOR. Poor kid has some real problems. Her marriage isn't working, she feels lousy about herself, she wants to start a business career. And she really needed a good cry.

HONEY. Oh God, I'll call her right away.

JUNIOR. *Not necessary.* Her father took care of it.

HONEY. He *did?*

JUNIOR. You think the only thing I fix is *drinks?* *(HE hands her a drink.)*

HONEY. Is that all you're going to tell me?

JUNIOR. I'll tell you lots of stuff, *later.* You'll be nauseatingly happy about it.

HONEY. What do you have planned for *now?*

JUNIOR. I just thought I'd let things happen.

HONEY. (*Holding up her glass in a toast.*) Happy anniversary.

JUNIOR. Right, forty great years. And here's to the next forty. (*HE clinks her glass. THEY drink.*) Excuse me. (*HE puts his glass down, walks to the stairs and leaps two at once. HE turns the speaker knob on. We hear "their song."*)

HONEY. Mmm, my favorite song.

JUNIOR. Yeah, how about that? (*HE flips a wall light switch off.*) Our "passional anthem."

HONEY. That's a coincidence.

JUNIOR. No, that's payola. (*HE flips a second wall switch.*) Fifty bucks and they play it all night long. (*HE walks toward her with a confident smile.*) Come here.

HONEY. (*SHE rises.*) Oh oh, should I scream for help?

JUNIOR. Not too loud, you'll wake the kids. Could you handle a few non-smartass words from your husband?

HONEY. Try me.

JUNIOR. I want to thank you for being my sweetheart ... even when I didn't deserve it, and for giving me the strength I never thought I'd find again.

HONEY. I can handle that, you marvelous pain in the ass. (*SHE kisses HIM.*)

JUNIOR. (*Sexily.*) *Great.* Now ... (*From Don Juan to Woody Allen.*) Could you carry me into the bedroom?

(*HONEY howls with laughter, JUNIOR swirls her in a
    dance. HE dips her deeply and THEY continue dancing
    as the MUSIC swells.*)

CURTAIN

COSTUME PLOT

Since this is a "romantic comedy" it is important to keep the characters looking attractive and pleasantly "fun" to the eye. Think CRUISEWEAR with each individual character dressing with that idea in their mind.

JUNIOR: Casual yachtsman, elegant, under-stated-Brooks Brothers relaxed.

HONEY: Elegant, vibrant yet soft.

STEPHANIE: Great sense of style with class, yet fun.

SCOTT: "Princeton" prep.

ARNIE: Midwestern tastes with a little California surf thrown in.

LIZ: Pragmatic with a message: Classic, no frills-Eddie Bauer look.

HONEY
Suit & blouse
Dressy evening dress
Pants or skirt
Sweatsuit
3 tops (optional)
Pumps or dress sandal

JUNIOR
Suit
Check pants
Blue sweater
2 shirts,
Dress shirt
Letter Sweater (U)

Pants—khaki
Loafers

STEPHANIE
Dressy dress
Elegant sweater & skirt
Jeans & silk blouse
Mink jacket

LIZ
Jogging suit
Running shoes
Cause T-shirt
Slip
Dressy dress
Russian T-shirt
Shorts & tee-top
Pumps

ARNIE
Sweatsuit
Boxer shorts & T-shirt
Seersucker sports coat and pants
Dress shirt
T-shirt (beach type)
Running shoes
Khakis or jeans
Sportshirt
Loafers & running shoes

SCOTT
Dress pants, sports coat

Dress shirt
Princeton T and running shorts
Khakis or gray jeans
Polo shirt
Sports shirt & green sweater
Loafers and running shoes

Note: Bold items are necessary to script.

PROPERTY PLOT

2 life jackets (Honey and Junior)
Carry-on satchel for pillow
1 bottle of Stolichnaya
Brochures on St. Petersburg
Small neck pillow (Honey and Junior)
5 brown plastic pill bottles (in Honey's purse)
Aspirin bottle
Cigarette and lighter Junior)
2 carry-on bags (Honey and Junior)
2 or 3 small suitcases (Liz and Arnie)
Nightshirt with pocket in Slumbertown lingerie box
    (Scott)
3 fanny packs (Stephanie)
Shopping bag "Copenhagen" (Stephanie)
Stocked bar with vodka, tonic, glasses, etc.
Fat-clogged arteries article from *American Health* (Liz)
Pink "Good & Plenty" ("terminator pill") (Junior)
Gift box with Captain's hat and note in it
Comb, perfume bottle (Stephanie)
Toothbrush (Arnie)
Jewelry box (Stephanie)
Ice bucket (2)
Small plastic bride and groom (Liz)
Electric cordless razor (Arnie)
2 green-wrapped mints (Junior)
Book: "X Rate Your Heart Attack"
2 brandy glasses filled with brandy
Newsweek and *Vogue*
Wad of dollar bills (Scott)
Small hand-held oxygen tank
Plate of tea sandwiches (Arnie)
Bags and packages from Copenhagen (Stephanie)
Binaca mouth spray (Liz)

University of Oslo sweatshirt (Scott)
Pill box (Junior)
2 pairs Mink earmuffs, 1 for wearing, 1 for dunking
Pulse timer watch (Scott)
Sport watch (Honey)
35mm camera with working flash (Liz)
Small portable typewriter (Arnie)
Pad and pencil (Liz)
Plate of pastries (Arnie)
Small tape recorder/player (Honey)
Paperback novel (Honey)
White handkerchief (Junior)
Russian chocolate bar (Liz)

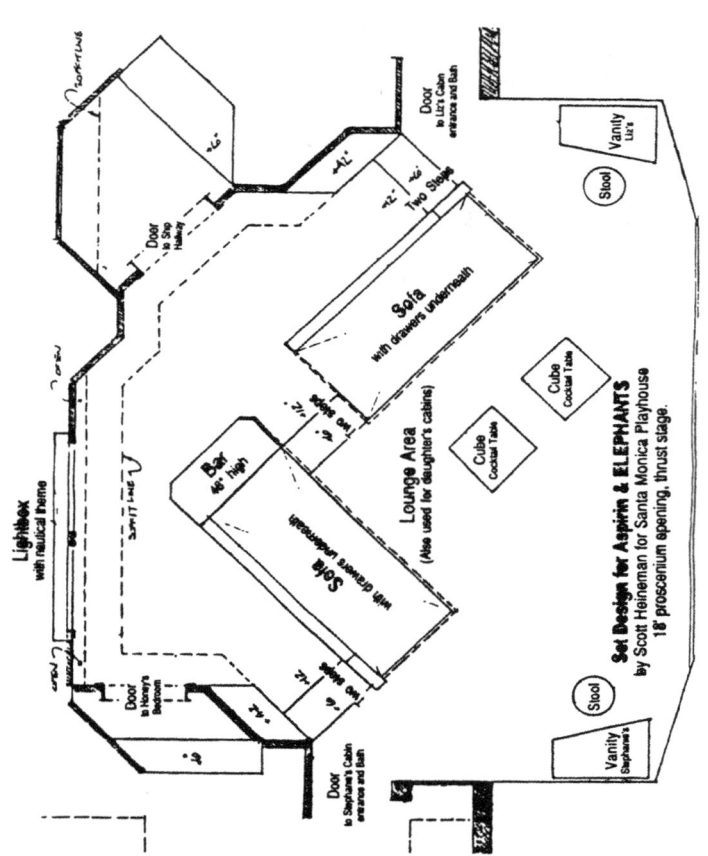

Set Design for Aspirin & ELEPHANTS
by Scott Heineman for Santa Monica Playhouse
18' proscenium opening, thrust stage.

NO SEX PLEASE, WE'RE BRITISH
Anthony Marriott and Alistair Foot

Farce / 7 m., 3 f. / Int.

A young bride who lives above a bank with her husband who is the assistant manager, innocently sends a mail order off for some Scandinavian glassware. What comes is Scandinavian pornography. The plot revolves around what is to be done with the veritable floods of pornography, photographs, books, films and eventually girls that threaten to engulf this happy couple. The matter is considerably complicated by the man's mother, his boss, a visiting bank inspector, a police superintendent and a muddled friend who does everything wrong in his reluctant efforts to set everything right, all of which works up to a hilarious ending of closed or slamming doors. This farce ran in London over eight years and also delighted Broadway audiences.

"Titillating and topical."
-NBC TV

"A really funny Broadway show."
-ABC TV

TREASURE ISLAND
Ken Ludwig

All Groups / Adventure / 10m, 1f (doubling) / Areas
Based on the masterful adventure novel by Robert Louis Stevenson, *Treasure Island* is a stunning yarn of piracy on the tropical seas. It begins at an inn on the Devon coast of England in 1775 and quickly becomes an unforgettable tale of treachery and mayhem featuring a host of legendary swashbucklers including the dangerous Billy Bones (played unforgettably in the movies by Lionel Barrymore), the sinister two-timing Israel Hands, the brassy woman pirate Anne Bonney, and the hideous form of evil incarnate, Blind Pew. At the center of it all are Jim Hawkins, a 14-year-old boy who longs for adventure, and the infamous Long John Silver, who is a complex study of good and evil, perhaps the most famous hero-villain of all time. Silver is an unscrupulous buccaneer-rogue whose greedy quest for gold, coupled with his affection for Jim, cannot help but win the heart of every soul who has ever longed for romance, treasure and adventure.

THE SCENE
Theresa Rebeck

Little Theatre / Drama / 2m, 2f / Interior Unit Set
A young social climber leads an actor into an extra-marital affair, from which he then creates a full-on downward spiral into alcoholism and bummery. His wife runs off with his best friend, his girlfriend leaves, and he's left with… nothing.

"Ms. Rebeck's dark-hued morality tale contains enough fresh insights into the cultural landscape to freshen what is essentially a classic boy-meets-bad-girl story."
- New York Times

"Rebeck's wickedly scathing observations about the sort of self-obsessed New Yorkers who pursue their own interests at the cost of their morality and loyalty."
- New York Post

"The Scene is utterly delightful in its comedic performances, and its slowly unraveling plot is thought-provoking and gut-wrenching."
- Show Business Weekly